Welcome to Christmas Sl
By Sarah]

Welcome Letter

Dear Holiday Dreamer,

Welcome to your cozy corner of Christmas magic! Pull up your fluffiest blanket, grab your favorite hot chocolate (extra marshmallows recommended!), and get ready for an adventure that's as unique as you are. You're holding more than just a book; you're holding sixteen doorways to wonder, courage, and discovery.

You know that feeling when snowflakes start falling and everything feels possible? That's exactly where these stories live. Whether you're curled up in your reading nook, snuggled in your favorite chair, or wrapped in that super-soft blanket you love, you're about to meet girls just like you who are finding their sparkle during the most magical time of the year.

These Christmas stories aren't about perfect girls having perfect holidays. They're about real girls: who sometimes say the wrong thing, who worry about fitting in, who aren't always brave but show up anyway. Girls who are figuring out their own kind of magic, even when things get messy.

Think of this book as your holiday bestie: the friend who gets it, won't judge, and reminds you that you're already amazing, exactly as you are. Whether you're dealing with friendship drama, family stuff, or just trying to survive December without accidentally setting the advent calendar on fire , these stories are here to remind you that you're not alone.

So grab your coziest blanket, your favorite snack (cookies totally count as dinner when you're reading, I don't make the rules), and dive into some holiday magic. Because the best kind of Christmas spirit isn't about being perfect—it's about being perfectly, wonderfully, authentically YOU. You've got this, and I've got your back.

With hot chocolate and holiday vibes,
Your Fellow Holiday Dreamer

P.S.—If you're reading this under the covers with a flashlight because you're supposed to be sleeping... I totally approve. The best stories are worth staying up for!

COPYRIGHT © 2025 By Sarah Bennett
All rights reserved.
No part of this publication may be reproduced, stored in a retrieval system, or transmitted in any form or by any means electronic, mechanical, photocopying, recording, or otherwise without the prior written permission of the publisher or the author.

How This Book Works
(Your Guide to Holiday Magic & Self-Discovery)

THE SETUP: These stories are divided into four magical sections:
- CHRISTMAS COURAGE: For when you need a little bravery boost
- HOLIDAY HEARTS & HOME: Because family drama hits different during December
- SANTA'S HELPERS: Finding your way to give back (even if you're super shy!)
- CHRISTMAS WISHES & WINTER WONDERS: Dream big, sparkle hard

READING TIME: Each story takes about 10-15 minutes to read—perfect for:
- Before bed (when your brain won't shut up)
- During lunch break (when you need an escape)
- Anytime you need a confidence boost

MAKING IT YOURS
- Read in order or jump around—you're the boss!
- Favorite parts? Underline them! (It's your book, make it messy!)
- Share with friends or keep it as your secret power source
- Come back to stories when you need them most

THE REAL DEAL: This isn't just a book—it's like having a bunch of older sisters sharing their stories and saying "Hey, we've been there, and you're doing amazing!" Every story is meant to remind you that:
- Your feelings are valid
- Your struggles are normal
- Your dreams matter
- Your version of magic counts

✧·° DEDICATION ·° ✧
To every girl who's ever...
Whispered her dreams to Christmas stars
Hidden her magic behind shy smiles
Wondered if anyone else feels this way
And kept hoping anyway
This book is for you.
And especially for my niece Emma,
who taught me that the best kind of magic
doesn't come from being perfect—
it comes from being perfectly, wonderfully you.
Keep sparkling, keep dreaming, keep believing.
Your story is just beginning.
✧·° With love and Christmas magic ·° ✧

CONTENTS

Welcome Letter
How This Book Works
Dedication

SECTION 1: CHRISTMAS COURAGE: Finding Your Inner Light
1. The Nutcracker's Understudy
2. North Pole News Network
3. Christmas Card Confessions
4. The Midnight Mass Solo

SECTION 2: HOLIDAY HEARTS & HOME: Where Family Gets Real
5. Two Christmas Eves
6. The Exchange Student's First Christmas
7. Gingerbread Legacy
8. The 12 Days of Friendship

SECTION 3: SANTA'S HELPERS: Making Magic For Others
9. The Christmas Tree Lot Teacher
10. Reindeer Games at Rainbow Retirement
11. The Elf Workshop Emergency
12. Mistletoe Market Miracles

SECTION 4: CHRISTMAS WISHES & WINTER WONDERS: Where Dreams Take Flight
13. Snowbound at Santa's Workshop
14. The Christmas Star Project
15. The Santa Cup Chaos
16. The Polar Express Promise

Final Thoughts
About the Author

SECTION 1: CHRISTMAS COURAGE

Finding Your Inner Light.
Hey there, holiday dreamer!

Picture this: You're curled up in your favorite reading spot. Maybe there's snow falling outside your window, or perhaps you're wrapped in that super-soft blanket you love. The Christmas lights are twinkling, casting little shadows that dance across your walls, and everything feels possible.

That's exactly where these stories live—in that magical space between what is and what could be.

You know that butterfly feeling you get before doing something brave? The one that mixes nerves with excitement until you can't tell them apart? Our four heroines know it well.

These aren't just stories about Christmas—they're about finding your spark when the world feels a little too dark, about standing up when it's easier to sit down, and about discovering that the best kind of magic often comes from being brave enough to be yourself.

And yes, there might be a few terrible dad jokes, one possibly sentient fruitcake, and a Christmas tornado along the way. After all, courage doesn't mean we can't have fun while being brave!

So grab that hot chocolate (extra marshmallows, obviously), get comfortable, and prepare to dive into four tales that might just change the way you see yourself this holiday season. Because here's the truth—you already have everything you need to be extraordinary. Sometimes it just takes a little Christmas courage to let that light shine.

And between you and me? The best stories always start with a girl who decides to be brave.

P.S.—Fair warning: These stories may cause spontaneous bursts of confidence, unexpected smiling, and an irresistible urge to chase your dreams. Side effects might include believing in yourself and realizing just how amazing you already are.

CHAPTER 1
The Nutcracker's Understudy

Lily Martinez's hands wouldn't stop shaking as she laced up her pointe shoes in the corner of the dance studio. The familiar scent of rosin and polish filled the air, mixing with the pine garland decorating the mirrors for the upcoming Nutcracker performance. Outside, fat snowflakes drifted past the tall windows, but inside, her forehead was already dotted with sweat.

"Five minutes until rehearsal, everyone!" Mrs. Chen, the artistic director, called out as she swept into the room in her signature black turtleneck.

Lily's stomach clenched. Even as an understudy for Clara, she still had to practice the main sequences. Just thinking about dancing in front of everyone made her heart race. She closed her eyes and tried the breathing exercise her therapist had taught her: in for four counts, hold for four, out for four.

"Hey, you okay?" Sophie, her best friend and fellow corps member, plopped down beside her. "You look a little pale."

"Just the usual," Lily managed a weak smile. "Trying not to throw up before rehearsal."

Sophie squeezed her hand. "You've got this. Besides, you're just the understudy. Rachel's been Clara for three years running—she could probably dance it in her sleep."

As if summoned by her name, Rachel Gibson glided past them, already in character with her perfect posture and serene smile. Her long blonde hair was twisted into an immaculate bun, not a single strand out of place. Lily touched her own dark curls, which refused to stay confined no matter how many bobby pins she used.

"Places for the party scene!" Mrs. Chen clapped her hands. "And Lily, dear, please try to relax your shoulders this time. You look like you're preparing for battle rather than a Christmas celebration."

A few giggles rippled through the studio. Lily felt her cheeks burn as she took her position. The opening notes of Tchaikovsky filled the room, and she forced herself to move. Each step felt mechanical, her anxiety building with every turn. When she caught glimpses of herself in the mirror, all she could see were her mistakes: shoulders too tense, arms not soft enough, smile more grimace than joy.

In the corner of the studio stood the old prop nutcracker, waiting to be used in the second act. It had been part of the studio's productions for decades, its painted uniform faded and chipped. Sometimes, during water breaks, Lily would find herself drawn to it. There was something comforting about its steady gaze and permanent smile, like it held all the secrets of past performances in its wooden heart.

✧

Dancing hadn't always been about anxiety for Lily. Her earliest memories were of twirling in her abuela's kitchen in Chicago, the smell of cinnamon and vanilla filling the air as Christmas cookies baked in the oven. *Bailarina pequeña* her grandmother would call her, eyes twinkling as three-year-old Lily attempted wobbly pirouettes in her sock feet.

By age seven, she was begging for real ballet lessons. Her parents had scraped together the money, working extra shifts—Mom at the hospital as a nurse, Dad taking on additional accounting clients. "Dance is expensive," they'd warned her, "so you have to be sure."

Lily had been sure. More than sure. That first time she'd stepped into Miss Katie's beginner ballet class, something had clicked into place. Here was a language her body understood instinctively: the arithmetic of rhythm, the geometry of movement, the poetry of motion. She'd advanced quickly, earning a spot in the junior company by age twelve.

The anxiety hadn't started until last year, creeping in slowly like a shadow at sunset. Maybe it was the pressure of moving to the senior company or watching dancers her age already landing major roles. Or perhaps it was the whispers she sometimes caught: "talented, but too nervous," "beautiful lines, if only she'd relax," "not quite what we look for in a principal dancer."

Still, in her bedroom late at night, Lily would close her eyes and allow herself to dream. She imagined herself on bigger stages—New York, London, Paris. In these private moments, she danced freely, unburdened by others' expectations or her own fears. The dream of dancing professionally remained her secret heart's wish, one she barely dared voice aloud.

Her mom had once found her old diary from when she was ten, filled with drawings of ballerinas and stage designs. On one page, in wobbly handwriting, young Lily had written: "When I dance, it feels like my soul has wings." Sometimes, in rare perfect moments during rehearsal, she could still find that feeling—when the music and movement became one, when her body remembered what her anxious mind forgot: she was born to dance.

The music swelled, and Lily's foot slipped slightly during a pirouette. Her heart hammered against her ribs as the familiar tightness crept into her chest. Not now, she pleaded silently, please not another panic attack now.

"Stop!" Mrs. Chen's voice cut through the music. "Lily, you're not connecting with the choreography at all. This is a joyful Christmas party, not a funeral march. Watch Rachel's expression—see how she embodies Clara's excitement?"

Rachel demonstrated the sequence again, her movements fluid and effortless. Lily felt her throat tightening, but then something unexpected happened. As Rachel spun past her, she gave Lily a small, genuine smile—not her usual stage smile, but something surprisingly kind.

"You know," Rachel whispered during their next formation, "I used to get so nervous, I'd forget my own name. My first year as Clara, I actually danced with my shoes on the wrong feet for half a rehearsal."

The mental image was so ridiculous that Lily couldn't help but giggle, some of the tension melting from her shoulders. Maybe perfect Rachel wasn't so perfect after all.

During their water break, Lily drifted toward the old nutcracker prop. Its familiar presence helped calm her racing thoughts. As she reached out to straighten its crooked hat, something strange happened. The wooden surface felt warm beneath her fingers, almost alive. For a brief moment, the studio seemed to shimmer, and she could have sworn she saw a flash of other dancers—girls in outdated practice clothes, all standing where she stood, all reaching for the same nutcracker with the same nervous expressions she often wore.

"Alright, everyone!" Mrs. Chen's voice snapped Lily back to reality. "Let's run the snow scene. Rachel, take the lead. Lily, watch carefully."

But before they could begin, Rachel landed awkwardly from a simple warm-up jump. The crack that followed seemed to echo through the studio, followed by Rachel's cry of pain.

"My ankle!" Rachel clutched her leg, her face pale. "Something's wrong. It—it doesn't feel right."

The studio erupted into chaos. Mrs. Chen rushed to Rachel's side while someone called for an ice pack. Sophie grabbed her phone to call Rachel's parents. And Lily stood frozen, the nutcracker's warmth still tingling in her fingertips as the reality of what this might mean began to sink in.

11

The next few days passed in a blur. Rachel's diagnosis—a severe ankle sprain—meant she would be out for the entire Christmas season. With only two weeks until opening night, Mrs. Chen made the announcement Lily had been both dreading and expecting.

"Lily will take over as Clara," Mrs. Chen declared during their emergency company meeting. Her tone left no room for discussion. "Sophie will move up to understudy."

That evening, Lily stayed late at the studio, claiming she wanted to practice. In reality, she needed somewhere to let her panic attack wash over her without her parents hovering anxiously. She sat in the dim studio, her back against the mirror, trying to remember how to breathe.

"I can't do this," she whispered to the empty room. "I'm not Rachel. I'm not ready."

The old nutcracker stood in its corner, its painted eyes somehow kinder in the fading light. Almost without thinking, Lily crawled over to it. As soon as her hand touched its wooden chest, that strange warmth returned. This time, the shimmer in the air was stronger.

A girl in a 1980s leotard appeared, transparent as mist. She was crying in the exact spot where Lily sat now. The vision shifted—another girl, this one from perhaps the 1990s, marking her steps alone, her face drawn with worry. More images flickered: dancers through the decades, all holding this same nutcracker, all facing their own fears.

The last image was the clearest—a young dancer who looked remarkably like Mrs. Chen, back when her hair was still jet black. She too clutched the nutcracker, her expression a mirror of Lily's current distress.

The visions faded, but the warmth remained. Lily realized she wasn't alone in this struggle. Every Clara before her had faced her own battles, her own doubts. They had all survived. Some had even triumphed.

Her phone buzzed with a text from Sophie: "You've got this. Want to come over tomorrow morning? Mom's making her famous Christmas cookies, and we can practice the party scene together. No pressure, just fun."

Another text followed, surprising her even more. It was from Rachel: "The physio says I'll be back for spring shows. Until then, the role is yours. You dance with more heart than anyone I know—when you forget to be afraid. Let's talk tomorrow? I have some tips that might help."

Lily looked up at the nutcracker, its smile seemingly wider in the growing darkness. "You've been watching over all of us, haven't you?" she whispered. "Every nervous Clara, every scared understudy..."

For the first time since Rachel's injury, Lily felt something other than panic. It wasn't confidence exactly—not yet—but perhaps the beginning of courage.

The next morning, Rachel sat in the studio's corner, her elevated ankle wrapped in a compression bandage, as she watched Lily practice. Despite her injury, Rachel had shown up every day for the past week, offering quiet guidance and unexpected friendship.

"You're thinking too much," Rachel called out as Lily marked through the Christmas party scene. "Remember what Mrs. Chen always says—feel the music in your bones."

Lily paused, pushing back a loose curl. "How do you make it look so effortless?"

Rachel's laugh was surprisingly self-deprecating. "Effortless? I threw up before every performance my first year. But you know what helped?" She pointed to the old nutcracker. "That guy right there. It became my pre-show ritual—touching its hand for luck."

Lily didn't mention the visions she'd seen, the warming sensation. Some magic, she felt, was meant to be kept secret.

The days flew by in a whirlwind of rehearsals. Lily's anxiety didn't disappear, but it changed shape. Instead of a crushing weight, it became more like a flutter of butterflies—still present, but almost energizing. The nutcracker continued to warm beneath her touch, showing her glimpses of past performances, each one carrying its own lesson.

Finally, opening night arrived. Backstage was chaos—corps members adjusting ribbons, stage moms helping with last-minute costume fixes, the buzz of excitement and nerves filling the air. Lily stood in her Clara costume, feeling both terrified and strangely calm.

She made her way to the old nutcracker, now in its place stage left. As she touched its hand, the warmth spread up her arm, and the clearest vision yet appeared: all the past Claras she'd seen, dancing together, their movements flowing into one another like a river of shared dreams and conquered fears. They turned to her, smiling, welcoming her into their dance.

"One minute to places!" the stage manager called.

Lily took her position. Her heart was racing, but this time it felt different. The music began, and she started to dance. Not perfectly—she could feel where her movements weren't quite precise, where her nerves showed through. But something magical was happening all the same.

She was dancing with her whole heart, letting the audience see not just the steps but the joy beneath them. When she faltered slightly during a turn, she kept going, remembering all those other dancers who had done the same. In the wings, she caught glimpses of Rachel nodding approvingly, of Sophie beaming, of Mrs. Chen watching with shining eyes.

The nutcracker seemed to glow faintly throughout the performance, visible only to her. Its presence reminded her that perfection wasn't the goal—courage was.

As the final notes faded and the curtain fell, Lily realized something profound: she hadn't conquered her anxiety completely, but she had learned to dance with it, to let it be part of her story rather than the end of it. The audience's applause thundered, and as she took her bow, she felt that childhood feeling again—of her soul having wings.

Later, after the flowers and congratulations, after her parents' fierce hugs and her friends' excited chatter, Lily returned to the quiet stage. The old nutcracker stood in its place, its painted smile as enigmatic as ever.

"Thank you," she whispered, touching its wooden hand one last time. The warmth that spread through her fingers felt like a promise—of more performances to come, of fears faced, of magic that lived in the heart of every dancer who dared to try.

CHAPTER 2
North Pole News Network

Sophie Davis sat in her bedroom, staring at the podcast microphone she'd saved six months of allowance to buy. Its sleek silver surface reflected the twinkling Christmas lights she'd strung around her desk, making it look almost magical in the early December darkness. She pressed the record button, then stopped. Pressed it again, stopped again.

"Come on, Sophie," she whispered to herself. "J-j-just do it."

The stutter that had followed her since childhood seemed to mock her dream of becoming a broadcaster. But the news about Madison High's holiday programs potentially being cut had lit a fire in her that burned stronger than her fear. Someone had to tell the story, and maybe that someone needed to be her.

She glanced at the bulletin board above her desk, covered with newspaper clippings and printouts of her favorite journalists. Among them was a Post-it note with her dad's handwriting: "The story matters more than how you tell it." He'd given her that note after she'd come home crying in eighth grade, when Bella Martinez had mimicked her stutter during her class presentation about the school's recycling program.

Sophie took a deep breath and pressed record again. "H-h-hi, this is S-Sophie Davis, and you're listening to..." She stopped, frustrated tears pricking at her eyes. The microphone seemed to dim slightly, as if disappointed.

Her phone buzzed with a text from her best friend, Maya: "Did you hear? They're voting on the budget cuts next week! The whole winter concert, the gift drive for the shelter, even the senior citizen tea party—all of it could be gone!"

Sophie's hands tightened around the microphone. The winter programs weren't just about holiday fun—they were the heart of their community. The concert raised money for music scholarships, the gift drive helped dozens of local families, and the tea party was the only Christmas celebration many elderly residents attended.

She thought about Mrs. O'Malley, who played piano for the concert every year, her arthritic fingers still dancing across the keys. About the kindergartners who made cards for the senior citizens, their wobbly letters full of love. About her little brother Tommy, who'd been practicing "Silent Night" on his violin for months.

The microphone in her hands suddenly felt warm, almost alive. Sophie blinked, wondering if she was imagining the soft golden glow emanating from its surface. Without thinking, she pressed record again.

"This is Sophie Davis," she said, forgetting to worry about her stutter, "and something important is happening at Madison High. Our holiday programs—the ones that have brought our town together for twenty-five years—might disappear. But before the school board votes, they need to hear the real story. The story of what these programs mean to all of us."

To her amazement, the words flowed smoothly when she spoke from her heart. Her stutter was still there, but it seemed to matter less. The microphone glowed brighter, as if responding to her authenticity.

Then she tried to say something she thought would sound more professional, and the microphone went dark and silent. No matter what she did, it wouldn't record.

"What in the world?" Sophie muttered, checking the batteries. The moment she stopped trying to sound like someone else, the microphone sprang back to life, glowing warmly in her hands.

Outside her window, snow began to fall, adding to the festive atmosphere that still clung to Madison despite the budget threat. Sophie wrapped her red and green plaid scarf around her neck, grabbed her magical microphone, and headed out into the December evening.

The town square looked like a scene from a snow globe. White lights twinkled in every shop window, and the massive community Christmas tree sparkled in front of the courthouse. Usually, the high school choir would be practicing here for their annual carol-singing fundraiser. Now the square felt too quiet, the silence heavy with what might be lost.

"S-sophie!" A small voice called out. Tommy came running across the square, violin case bouncing against his back, leaving footprints in the fresh snow. "Did you really s-start a podcast? Can I be on it?"

She smiled at her little brother, whose stutter matched her own—a family trait that their mom called their "unique rhythm." "Actually, yeah. Want to t-tell everyone about your violin piece?"

The microphone glowed as Tommy spoke earnestly about practicing "Silent Night" every day after school. "It's for Mrs. Jensen at the senior center," he explained. "She told me last year it was her mom's favorite Christmas song, and she m-misses hearing it."

As if drawn by Tommy's story, other people began approaching. Mr. Chen from the bakery talked about donating cookies to the tea party every year. A group of seniors from the high school described their tradition of dressing as elves to deliver gifts to the shelter.

The microphone seemed to know exactly when someone was speaking their truth. It would glow brightest during the most heartfelt moments, dim during rehearsed speeches, and completely shut off if anyone tried to exaggerate or be fake.

Sophie's stutter became less noticeable as she conducted interviews, too caught up in the stories to worry about her speech. The magic of the microphone seemed to wrap around her like a warm Christmas blanket, giving her courage she didn't know she had.

"Would you like to share your perspective?" she asked Principal Matthews, spotting him hanging wreaths outside the school entrance.

He hesitated, then spoke about the district's financial struggles. The microphone dimmed slightly. But when he added, "Though honestly, seeing the teenagers serve tea to our senior citizens every year reminds me why I became an educator," the microphone blazed with golden light.

Back home that evening, Sophie edited her first podcast episode while drinking hot chocolate topped with candy cane marshmallows. Her mom poked her head in, the scent of gingerbread following her from the kitchen.

"How's the reporting going, sweetheart?"

"It's... different than I expected," Sophie replied, noticing she hadn't stuttered. "I thought I needed to sound like the reporters on TV, but this m-microphone..." She paused, wondering how to explain its magic. "It's teaching me something about truth."

As December progressed, *North Pole News Network* gained listeners faster than Sophie could have imagined. Her podcast notifications chimed like Christmas bells every time someone shared a new story. But it wasn't just about numbers—something magical was happening in Madison.

People began talking about the holiday programs differently. Instead of focusing on budget sheets and costs, they shared memories and meanings. The local coffee shop started playing episodes over their speakers, the sound of Sophie's voice mixing with the scent of peppermint lattes and evergreen wreaths.

But not everyone was supportive. One evening, as Sophie was editing her latest episode, a notification popped up on her phone. Bella Martinez, who ran the school's official social media accounts, had posted: "Who wants to listen to a podcast where the host can't even talk properly?"

The words hit Sophie like a physical blow. She pushed away from her desk, her chest tight. The Christmas lights above her bed blurred as tears filled her eyes. Years of speech therapy, countless hours of practice, and still, her stutter made her a target. Maybe Bella was right—who would want to listen to her?

In her bedroom that night, Sophie buried her face in her pillow, letting the tears fall silently. All the confidence she'd built over the past weeks seemed to crumble. She grabbed her phone, finger hovering over the 'Delete Podcast' button. All her episodes, all those stories she'd collected—maybe they'd be better told by someone else, someone whose words didn't trip and stumble.

Through her tears, she noticed the microphone on her desk beginning to pulse with a warm, steady light—like a heartbeat. The gentle glow reminded her of every person who'd trusted her with their story: Tommy with his violin dreams, Mrs. O'Malley with her piano memories, the shelter director with his quiet hope. Each of them had shared something real with her, not because she spoke perfectly, but because she listened perfectly.

Sophie reached out and touched the microphone, feeling its familiar warmth surge through her fingers and into her heart. She sat up, wiped her eyes, and pressed record.

"You know what?" she said, her voice clear despite her stutter, "My s-speech might not be perfect, but my stories are true. And sometimes the m-most important voices are the ones that have to work the hardest to be heard."

The microphone glowed brighter with each word, as if confirming that authenticity mattered more than perfection. Sophie posted her response and switched off her phone, choosing to focus instead on editing her latest episode about the senior center tea party. She had important stories to tell, and she was the only one who could tell them in exactly this way.

The night before the school board meeting, Sophie couldn't sleep. Tomorrow, she would have to speak in person—no magical microphone to help her, no editing software to smooth out her words. The Christmas lights in her room cast dancing shadows as she paced, practicing her speech.

Her phone buzzed. It was a voice message from Mrs. O'Malley: "Dear Sophie, I just listened to all your episodes. You reminded an old piano teacher that music isn't about perfection—it's about touching hearts. Your voice, my dear, with all its unique rhythms, is touching hearts."

More messages followed. Tommy's violin teacher sharing how many students were inspired by his interview. The shelter director describing donations increasing after people heard the podcast. Even Principal Matthews sent a link to a local news story about their small-town podcast making a big difference.

The morning of the meeting arrived with fresh snow and freezing temperatures, but the school board room was packed with warmth—both from bodies and Christmas spirit. Sophie clutched her microphone like a talisman, even though she couldn't use it. To her surprise, Bella Martinez slipped into the seat beside her.

"Hey," Bella whispered, looking uncomfortable. "I was wrong about...you know. Your podcast? It's actually pretty good. My grandma cried when she heard the story about the senior center tea party."

Before Sophie could respond, the board chairman called her name. As she walked to the podium, her heartbeat thundering in her ears, something extraordinary happened. The magical microphone in her hand began to glow, its warmth spreading up her arm and into her chest, filling her with the collected courage of every person who'd trusted her with their story.

"M-my name is Sophie Davis," she began, her stutter present but no longer important. "And I'm here to tell you about the heart of Christmas in Madison..."

For the next ten minutes, Sophie spoke from her heart, her words sometimes flowing smooth as silk, sometimes catching and stumbling, but always true. She talked about Tommy's violin and Mrs. Jensen's memories, about teenage elves and senior citizens sharing tea and stories, about a community that measured its wealth not in dollars but in traditions and connections.

The microphone glowed brighter with each honest word, illuminating faces in the audience—faces that were smiling, nodding, some wiping away tears. Even the board members leaned forward, caught in the magic of pure truth being spoken from the heart.

When the board chairman announced their decision to maintain funding for the holiday programs through community partnerships and local business sponsorships, the room erupted in applause. But it was what he said next that made Sophie's microphone glow its brightest yet.

"And we'd like to offer one more solution," he smiled, adjusting his red-and-green striped tie. "Ms. Davis, would you consider turning your *North Pole News Network* into a permanent student media program? It seems our community needs its voice—all its unique voices—to be heard year-round."

That weekend, as the winter concert filled the auditorium with music, Sophie sat in the sound booth, her magical microphone capturing every note of Tommy's "Silent Night" performance. Her stutter hadn't disappeared, but somehow it had become part of her story rather than an obstacle to it.

Mrs. O'Malley's piano accompanied the choir, her arthritic fingers dancing across the keys as gracefully as ever. The senior citizens sat in their reserved front rows, Christmas corsages pinned to their coats—courtesy of the local florist who'd heard their stories on the podcast. Even Bella had volunteered to help, handling the social media coverage with a new appreciation for authentic storytelling.

As Sophie made her closing announcement for the evening, her magical microphone glowed softly in her hands. "This is Sophie Davis, r-reminding you that every voice matters, especially at Christmas. Sometimes the most beautiful stories aren't the most perfectly told—they're the ones told with heart. From all of us at North Pole News Network, m-merry Christmas, Madison."

The microphone's glow faded to a gentle shimmer, but Sophie knew its magic would always be there, reminding her that the truest voice is your own—stutter and all. Outside, snow fell softly on Madison's twinkling Christmas lights, and somewhere in the distance, she could have sworn she heard sleigh bells ring.

CHAPTER 3
Christmas Card Confessions

Maya Anderson sat cross-legged on her bed, surrounded by colored pencils, markers, and scraps of festive paper. Outside her frost-covered window, Christmas lights twinkled along their normally cheerful street, but this year they seemed to mock her family's empty bank account. The "For Sale" sign on Mr. Peterson's car next door reminded her too much of when Dad had to sell his own car last month.

Still, the faint glow from their small artificial Christmas tree (pulled from storage instead of their usual fresh tree tradition) mixed with the scent of the cinnamon cookies Mom was stress-baking downstairs made everything feel almost normal. Almost.

Maya picked up her sketchbook, flipping through the Christmas card designs she'd been working on. A snow-covered cottage with smoke curling from its chimney. A family of cardinals perched on a holly branch. A winter village scene that had taken her three hours to perfect.

"These are good," she whispered to herself, trying to believe it. Art had always been her escape, but now it needed to be more. It needed to be a solution.

The idea had come to her last night, after overhearing Mom and Dad's whispered conversation about "making Christmas special even without..." before their voices had trailed off into worried silence. Maya knew what they weren't saying. After Dad lost his job at the tech company, even simple gifts had become impossible.

A soft knock at her door interrupted her thoughts. "Maya? Hot chocolate delivery!" Her mom entered, carrying two steaming mugs topped with tiny marshmallows shaped like stars. Despite everything, Mom still found ways to add magic to small moments.

"Thanks, Mom." Maya cleared a space among her art supplies. "These look fancy."

"Well, some things are worth celebrating," Mom said, settling beside her. "Like my talented daughter starting her own Christmas card business." Her smile was genuine, but Maya caught the worry in her eyes.

"I just hope people want to buy them," Maya mumbled, sipping her chocolate. "I know it won't fix everything, but maybe I could at least get small gifts for everyone?"

Her mother wrapped an arm around her shoulders. "Oh, sweetheart. You don't need to fix anything. Your father and I—"

"I want to help," Maya interrupted. "Besides, people still send real Christmas cards, right? Everyone's tired of digital everything."

Before her mother could respond, a golden sparkle caught Maya's eye. One of her blank cards seemed to shimmer in the afternoon light. She reached for it, and the paper felt warm beneath her fingers, like it had been sitting in sunlight instead of her cold bedroom.

"That's strange," she murmured, picking up her favorite drawing pen. As she began to sketch on the shimmering paper, something magical happened. The ink seemed to flow on its own, creating patterns more beautiful than anything she'd drawn before. When she added color, the pigments blended perfectly, creating depths and highlights she'd never managed to achieve.

"Maya, this is beautiful!" her mother gasped, watching the artwork come to life. "It looks like something from a fairy tale."

The finished card showed a simple scene: a girl hanging a star on a small Christmas tree while snow fell outside her window. But somehow, it captured exactly how Maya felt—the mixture of hope and sadness, of trying to create light in darker times.

"I think I know who needs this one," Maya said softly, thinking of Mrs. Harrison across the street. The elderly woman had lost her husband last spring, and Maya often saw her sitting alone by her window.

That evening, Maya slipped the card into Mrs. Harrison's mailbox. What she didn't know—not yet—was that when Mrs. Harrison would open the card the next morning, something extraordinary would happen.

The next morning, Maya was eating her cereal (the last of the Christmas-shaped marshmallow ones she'd been hoarding since November) when Mrs. Harrison appeared at their front door, tears streaming down her face. Maya's heart sank—had her card somehow made things worse?

"Oh, my dear girl," Mrs. Harrison sniffled, clutching Maya's card. "How did you know? When I opened this, I saw... I saw George and me decorating our first tree together. All those Christmases we shared..." She wiped her eyes, then surprised Maya with a warm hug. "It reminded me that it's okay to feel both sad and happy during the holidays. And..." She pulled back with a mysterious smile. "I have a proposition for you."

It turned out Mrs. Harrison had been a greeting card designer herself, back in the "stone age" as she jokingly called it. Her basement was filled with crafting supplies she no longer used. "Consider it your new art studio," she declared. "In exchange for keeping an old lady company during her afternoon tea."

"Deal!" Maya grinned. "As long as you promise not to make me try your infamous fruitcake."

"Cheeky! That fruitcake is a family treasure. It's only slightly older than I am."

As Maya set up her workspace in Mrs. Harrison's cozy basement, more orders started coming in. Word spread quickly in their small town, especially after Mrs. Harrison posted about Maya's cards on the community page (even though she consistently referred to it as "The Network" and kept accidentally adding angry face emojis instead of hearts).

Each card Maya created on the magical paper revealed something different to its recipient. Mr. Chen from the grocery store saw his daughter, away at college, missing his dumplings. The card for Maya's math teacher, Ms. Peters, showed her feeding stray cats behind the school—a secret act of kindness no one knew about.

Sometimes the revelations were funny. The card for Mr. Wilson, the grumpiest man on their street, showed him dancing to Christmas songs in his garage. He'd been so shocked that someone knew his secret that he'd actually cracked a smile—possibly his first since 1987.

But it was the card for Jenny Blake, the most popular girl in school, that really surprised Maya. When Jenny opened it, she saw herself sitting alone at lunch, just wishing someone would see past her perfect digital feed. The next day, Jenny joined Maya at her usual lunch table.

"Your card," Jenny whispered, picking at her salad. "How did you know I was so lonely?"

"Sometimes we all need someone to really see us," Maya replied, sharing her cookies (Mom's stress-baking had reached industrial levels). "Even if we look fine on the outside."

As December progressed, Maya's cards began weaving invisible threads through the community. Mrs. Harrison's basement turned into an unofficial gathering spot, with people dropping by to share stories and cookies (but never the fruitcake, which Maya was convinced was actually gaining sentience in its tin).

The magic worked in unexpected ways too. When Maya created a card for her dad, fighting back tears as she drew, the paper seemed to sparkle more than usual.

The card for her dad was different. As Maya drew, memories flooded the paper: Dad teaching her to ride a bike, his terrible dad jokes at breakfast, the way he still checked under her bed for monsters even though she was "way too old for that." The card shimmered so brightly she had to squint.

"Honey?" Mom called down the basement stairs. "Dad's home early. He seems... different."

Maya found her father in the kitchen, holding her card with trembling hands. His eyes were red, but he was smiling—really smiling—for the first time in months.

"When I opened this," he said softly, "I saw something amazing. I saw myself through your eyes, Maya. Not as someone who lost his job, but as your dad. Someone who still matters." He pulled out a chair. "And then the strangest thing happened. I got a call from Mr. Chen at the grocery store. His brother's art supply company needs a new accounting manager. He... he wants to interview me tomorrow."

Maya's heart soared. The magic was spreading in ways she hadn't expected, connecting people and opportunities like Christmas lights strung between houses.

✧

Over the next week, more miracle-like coincidences followed. Jenny's mom, a real estate agent, helped Mrs. Harrison finally sell her too-big house—but with the condition that Maya could keep using the basement studio in the new year. Ms. Peters' secret cat-feeding mission turned into a school-wide pet food drive. Even Mr. Wilson's garage dancing became a neighborhood joke-turned-tradition, with impromptu Christmas dance parties breaking out on their street.

But the real Christmas magic peaked at the community center's holiday gathering. Maya had created one final card—her masterpiece—for the whole town. As people passed it around, each person saw something different, yet connected: their shared struggles, their secret kindnesses, their hidden hopes.

Mr. Chen saw himself as the heart of the community, not just the grocery store owner. Jenny's mom realized her real estate work helped create homes, not just sell houses. Ms. Peters discovered her students admired her quiet compassion more than her perfect math lessons.

"Maya," her dad said, watching the scene unfold, "I think you've given everyone the most valuable gift this Christmas."

"What's that?" she asked, leaning against his shoulder.

"The gift of being truly seen." He squeezed her hand. "And speaking of gifts..." He pulled out an envelope. "My first paycheck came early. Want to help me do some last-minute shopping?"

Maya looked around the community center. Mrs. Harrison was teaching Jenny's little sister how to make paper snowflakes. Mr. Wilson was actually laughing at one of Dad's terrible jokes. Mom was sharing her cookie recipes (but still guarding her secret ingredient). The room glowed with warmth that had nothing to do with the fireplace.

"Actually," Maya smiled, "I think we already have everything we need."

She reached for her sketchbook, the pages now filled with orders for the new year. The magical paper sparkled faintly, but Maya realized something—maybe the real magic hadn't been in the paper at all. Maybe it had been in the simple act of taking time to really see people, to create something that showed them they weren't alone.

As if reading her thoughts, Mrs. Harrison winked at her from across the room. "You know what goes perfectly with all this Christmas joy?" she called out mischievously.

"Don't say fruitcake!" the entire room chorused, bursting into laughter.

Outside, snow began to fall, each flake carrying its own story, its own magic. Maya had started making cards to earn money for gifts, but she'd ended up giving her community something far more precious—the gift of connection. And that, she realized, was the greatest Christmas magic of all.

CHAPTER 4
The Midnight Mass Solo

Emma Taylor's fingers hovered over the ancient church piano's ivory keys, her breath creating small clouds in the cold December air. The empty sanctuary felt different in the early morning light—peaceful, expectant, as if the very walls were waiting for something extraordinary.

She glanced around to make sure she was truly alone, then pulled out her worn composition notebook. The pages were filled with songs she'd never dared to share, modern melodies interwoven with fragments of traditional hymns. Her latest piece was a contemporary arrangement of "O Holy Night" that had been haunting her dreams.

As she played the first few notes, something magical happened. The old piano seemed to wake up, its notes resonating with unusual warmth. Additional harmonies floated in beneath her melody, as if the piano was accompanying her all on its own. Emma's hands faltered, but the encouraging music continued, gently urging her back into the song.

"What do you think you're doing?"

The harsh voice shattered the moment. Katherine Morrison, the church's celebrated soloist for the past twenty years, stood in the doorway, her face pinched with disapproval. The piano's magical harmonies faded into silence.

"I was just... practicing," Emma stammered, quickly hiding her notebook.

"That didn't sound like the traditional arrangement." Katherine's heels clicked ominously against the wooden floor as she approached. "The Midnight Mass is not the time for... experimentations. We have standards to maintain."

Before Emma could respond, the church door burst open again. Mrs. Chen, the choir director, rushed in, looking uncharacteristically flustered. "Katherine, please, let's discuss this reasonably—"

"There's nothing to discuss," Katherine interrupted. "If you're seriously considering 'modernizing' our Christmas service, you'll have to do it without me. Twenty years of tradition, and now you want to throw it all away? I quit!"

The door slammed behind her, the sound echoing through the sanctuary like a judgment. Emma's heart sank as Mrs. Chen turned to her with an apologetic smile.

"Emma, dear... how would you feel about taking the solo for Midnight Mass?"

The world seemed to tilt sideways. "Me? But I... I can't... I mean, I've never..."

"You have a beautiful voice," Mrs. Chen said gently. "And more importantly, you have heart. Besides," she added with a twinkle in her eye, "I heard what you were playing just now. Perhaps it's time for some fresh perspectives on our old traditions."

Emma's protest was interrupted by the arrival of the children's choir for their morning practice. They tumbled in like a wave of holiday energy, candy cane residue still sticky on some of their faces.

"Where's Ms. Morrison?" little Sophie asked, her choir robe dragging on the ground. "She was supposed to help us with our part today."

Mrs. Chen's smile grew wider. "Actually, Emma will be working with you this morning. Won't you, Emma?"

Before Emma could flee in terror, Sophie grabbed her hand with sticky fingers. "Really? But you're not scary like Ms. Morrison! This is going to be so much better!"

The piano's keys glimmered briefly in the morning light, and through the stained-glass windows, the Christmas star seemed to wink at her. Emma took a deep breath, wondering if the tight feeling in her chest was panic or possibility.

"Okay, everyone," Emma said, trying to keep her voice steady as twelve eager faces looked up at her. "Let's start with—"

"Wait!" Seven-year-old Tommy waved his hand frantically. "We need our good luck ritual first!"

"Your... what?"

The children formed a circle, pulling Emma in with them. "Ms. Morrison always made us stand super straight and proper," Sophie explained, "but when she wasn't here, we did this instead." The kids started spinning, making quiet "whoosh" sounds. "We're a Christmas tornado!"

Emma couldn't help laughing, especially when Tommy got dizzy and wobbled into the piano. To her amazement, instead of the discordant crash she expected, the piano played a twinkling scale of notes, like musical laughter. The children froze, wide-eyed.

"Did the piano just... giggle?" Sophie whispered.

Before Emma could respond, a warm glow caught her attention. Her sheet music, peeking out of her notebook, was shimmering with a soft golden light. As she pulled it out, the children gathered around, their choir robes rustling.

"Those notes look like they're dancing," Tommy observed, pointing to where Emma had sketched her modern additions to the traditional carol.

Suddenly inspired, Emma sat at the piano. "What if we actually made them dance? Instead of just standing still during the song, what if we..." She played a few notes of "O Holy Night" with a gentle, swaying rhythm.

The children's faces lit up. Sophie started swaying naturally, and the hem of her choir robe sparkled like starlight. One by one, as the other children joined in, their robes began to shimmer too.

"Ms. Morrison said moving during sacred songs was disrespectful," a quiet girl named Lucy mentioned, though she was already swaying.

"Well," Emma found herself saying with unexpected confidence, "I think joy is the most respectful thing we can offer, especially at Christmas."

The ancient church bells chose that moment to chime the hour, and to everyone's astonishment, they rang in perfect harmony with Emma's modern arrangement. Even Mrs. Chen, who had been watching from the doorway, looked amazed.

Word spread quickly about the changes to the Christmas program. Not everyone was pleased. Emma overheard whispers after Sunday service, saw the concerned looks from elderly parishioners. Katherine Morrison had apparently started a "Save Our Sacred Songs" group on Facebook, which would have been more threatening if she hadn't accidentally used dancing Santa emojis in her angry posts.

But Emma had unexpected allies. Mr. Jenkins, the 80-year-old church groundskeeper, caught her practicing one evening. She braced for criticism, but he just smiled and said, "About time someone woke up that old piano. Been sleeping for twenty years, if you ask me."

During the next week's rehearsals, magical moments kept happening. The Christmas star in the stained-glass window would create a spotlight that followed Emma around the sanctuary. The piano continued to add its own harmonies when she practiced alone, sometimes even throwing in jazzy little riffs that made her giggle.

The children's choir was transforming too. Tommy, who used to hide behind taller kids, now insisted on standing front and center. Sophie discovered she could hit notes she never knew she had. Lucy's voice, once barely a whisper, grew stronger every day.

"Emma?" Lucy tugged on her sleeve after one practice. "Can we show you something?"

The children had created their own addition to the song—simple hand movements that made their robes shimmer like the northern lights. As they demonstrated, their pure voices blending perfectly with the new arrangement, Emma felt tears in her eyes.

The piano played a gentle encouragement, and through the stained glass, the Christmas star seemed to pulse in time with the music. This, Emma realized, was what Christmas magic felt like—not perfect performance, but pure joy.

Three days before Midnight Mass, disaster struck. During dress rehearsal, Emma's voice cracked on the high note she'd been dreading. Her confidence crumbled, and the children's robes stopped shimmering. Even the piano seemed to droop.

"Maybe Katherine was right," Emma whispered, fighting tears. "Maybe I'm not—"

"Emergency Christmas council!" Sophie announced, and before Emma could protest, the children formed a circle around her. Tommy produced a slightly squashed candy cane from his pocket.

"When I forget my words," he said solemnly, breaking it in half to share, "my mom says it's because I'm thinking too much about my brain and not enough about my heart."

"Tommy's right!" Lucy, who had finally found her voice, stepped forward. "Ms. Morrison always said we had to be perfect. But when you sing, Emma, you make us feel like it's okay to just be... us."

The piano suddenly played a few notes of "O Holy Night," but in a minor key that sounded surprisingly like Katherine Morrison's strict version. Then it shifted to Emma's arrangement, and the difference was clear—one was about perfection, the other about joy.

That evening, as Emma stayed late to practice, she heard footsteps. Katherine Morrison stood in the doorway, but something was different. She looked... smaller, somehow.

"I heard them today," Katherine said quietly. "The children. They... they sound happy."

Emma nodded, not trusting her voice.

"Twenty years ago," Katherine continued, sitting beside Emma on the piano bench, "I was just like you. I had my own arrangements, my own ideas. But everyone said tradition was more important. So, I learned to be perfect instead of authentic."

The piano played a soft, sympathetic chord.

"Would..." Emma hesitated. "Would you like to hear what I'm planning for Christmas Eve?"

As Emma played, something extraordinary happened. The sheet music began to glow, sending golden light dancing across Katherine's face. Through the stained glass, the Christmas star cast its spotlight on them both. And when Katherine began to sing harmony—hesitant at first, then stronger—their voices blended like they were always meant to find each other.

Christmas Eve arrived with snow and stars. The sanctuary was packed, glowing with candlelight. Emma peeked out from behind the curtain, her heart racing. The children's choir gathered around her, their robes already starting to shimmer with excitement.

"Remember," she told them, "we're not performing for them. We're sharing our joy."

The piano's keys glimmered encouragingly. Through the stained glass, the Christmas star seemed brighter than ever. And then, just before they walked out, Katherine appeared.

"Room for one more in this new tradition?" she asked, smoothing her choir robe.

The music began softly—the traditional opening everyone expected. But then Emma's voice lifted in her contemporary arrangement, and the children began their gentle movements, their robes shimmering like earthbound stars. The piano added its own magic, harmonies weaving through the ancient sanctuary like threads of gold.

When Katherine joined in, adding depth to the modern bridges between verses, audible gasps rippled through the congregation. The church bells chimed unexpectedly, perfectly in tune. Through the stained glass, the Christmas star cast its light on all of them—young and old, traditional and modern, blending together into something entirely new yet somehow timeless.

Mr. Jenkins later swore he saw actual angels joining in, though that might have been the eggnog talking. Mrs. Chen cried happy tears into her sheet music. Even the staunchest traditionalists were seen swaying slightly in their pews.

As the final notes faded, Emma realized something profound. The magic hadn't changed their voices—it had simply helped them find the courage to let their true voices be heard. The piano played a quiet, approving chord.

"Emma?" Sophie tugged at her robe after the service. "Can we do this again next year? Maybe with that song you wrote about the grumpy donkey at the nativity?"

Emma laughed, hugging her young protégé. "Why wait for next year? I think this church has room for new songs all year round."

The Christmas star twinkled in agreement, and somewhere in the distance, the church bells chimed a melody that sounded suspiciously like Emma's newest composition. After all, the best traditions aren't the ones that never change—they're the ones that grow with love, one voice, one heart, one song at a time.

SECTION 2: HOLIDAY HEARTS & HOME

Grab your fuzzy socks and that hot chocolate you've been saving (you know, the one with the mini candy canes and marshmallows), because you're about to dive into the most wonderfully chaotic, heartwarming, and totally relatable holiday stories ever!

Let's be real—December can be SUPER complicated when you're trying to figure out friend drama, family stuff, and why your cat keeps attacking the Christmas tree ornaments. (Spoiler alert: because cats gonna cat.) But it's also kind of amazing, right? Like when you're baking cookies at midnight with your bestie, or when your whole family is singing off-key to holiday songs in the car, and suddenly everything just feels... magical?

These stories are about girls just like you—dealing with friendship breakups and makeups, trying not to roll their eyes when Mom suggests another "family tradition" (but secretly loving it), and discovering that sometimes the most epic holiday moments happen when absolutely nothing goes according to plan.

You'll meet Isabella, who's learning that being yourself is actually the coolest trend ever. There's Grace, navigating friend group drama with the help of some seriously mysterious Christmas magic (and a slightly unhinged snowman). And don't forget Mei and Sarah, who prove that the best traditions are the ones you make up yourself—even if they involve a decoration-obsessed squirrel with surprisingly good taste.

So get cozy, ignore your homework for a bit (jk, do your homework... but maybe after one story?), and join us for some holiday magic. Whether you're dealing with bestie drama, family chaos, or just trying to survive December without accidentally setting the advent calendar on fire, these stories are here to remind you that you're not alone.

And hey, sometimes the most amazing memories come from those totally awkward, completely imperfect, absolutely unforgettable holiday moments.

P.S. Did I mention there's a squirrel who thinks he's an interior decorator? Because that's definitely a thing.

CHAPTER 5
Two Christmas Eves

Olivia Martinez stood in her bedroom, glaring at the two identical Christmas stockings laid out on her bed. One for Mom's house, one for Dad's. Because apparently, Christmas needed a backup copy this year.

"This is ridiculous," she muttered, stuffing her favorite holiday sweater (the one with a sloth wearing a Santa hat that said 'Slow Down, It's Christmas') into her overnight bag. At least she got to wear the same sweater to both celebrations. Though knowing her luck, she'd probably end up wearing it inside out at one house just to keep things different.

The snow globe on her dresser caught her eye—a gift from her grandmother last Christmas, back when the world made sense and holidays didn't need scheduling charts color-coded by parent. It was beautiful, featuring a tiny Victorian house with warm windows and a miniature family decorating a tree.

Olivia picked it up, giving it a frustrated shake. But instead of snow swirling around the usual scene, something strange happened. The globe filled with golden light, and suddenly she was looking at a Christmas memory that wasn't hers.

A little girl with her mother's eyes was helping her grandmother make tamales, laughing as masa dough covered every surface of a familiar kitchen—her mom's childhood kitchen. The scene shifted, and now a boy who looked suspiciously like her dad was attempting to untangle Christmas lights with his father, creating an even bigger knot while telling increasingly terrible dad jokes.

"Olivia?" Her mom's voice broke through her trance. "Have you packed? Your father will be here in twenty minutes."

"Coming!" Olivia quickly tucked the snow globe into her bag. She wasn't sure what had just happened, but she wasn't leaving this magical object behind.

Downstairs, her mom was stress-baking Christmas cookies—her third batch this week. The kitchen smelled like cinnamon and anxiety.

"Remember, Christmas Eve dinner is at your father's, then you're back here for Christmas morning, then—"

"Then back to Dad's for Christmas dinner, then here for December 26th breakfast," Olivia recited. "I know, Mom. I have the spreadsheet memorized. Though I still think Google Calendar wasn't meant to handle this much holiday drama."

Her mom's face softened. "I know this is different, sweetie. But we're trying to make sure you get the best of both—"

"Both Christmases?" Olivia tried to keep the edge out of her voice. "Because nothing says 'holiday magic' like celebrating everything twice?"

Before her mom could respond, the doorbell rang. Perfect timing, as always. Her dad stood on the porch, wearing his infamous reindeer tie that played "Rudolph the Red-Nosed Reindeer" when squeezed. Some embarrassing dad traditions, apparently, survived even divorce.

"Ready for Christmas Eve Eve Eve?" he asked with forced cheerfulness.

"That's not a thing, Dad."

"Sure it is! It's like Christmas Eve, but with 200% more Eve-ning entertainment!" He squeezed his tie for emphasis, and tinny electronic music filled the awkward silence.

Olivia rolled her eyes but couldn't completely hide her smile. The snow globe in her bag seemed to warm slightly, and she had an idea. Not a particularly nice idea, but definitely an interesting one. If everyone wanted two Christmases, maybe it was time to make things so complicated they'd have to go back to just one...

Olivia's *Operation Christmas Chaos* started small. She accidentally-on-purpose mixed up the Christmas cookie recipes, sending her dad's snickerdoodles to her mom's house and her mom's gingerbread to her dad's. But instead of confusion, both parents just called each other laughing.

"Remember that year I burned every batch?" her dad chuckled over speakerphone. "The smoke alarm played better Christmas music than my tie!"

The snow globe glowed warmly, showing teenage versions of her parents at a high school bake sale, her dad proudly presenting cookies that looked more like holiday-themed hockey pucks.

Her next plan involved "forgetting" essential decorations at each house. But when she left the star for Mom's tree at Dad's house, something magical happened. The snow globe swirled to life, showing her dad as a little boy, crafting a star from aluminum foil with his grandmother.

"Hey, Liv," he called out, rummaging through the attic. "Want to learn how to make an old-school tree topper? Your 36buela taught me this trick with foil and wire..."

An hour later, they had created a wonderfully wonky star that looked like it had been designed by elves who'd had too much hot chocolate. It was perfectly imperfect, just like their new normal.

At her mom's house, the forgotten ornaments led to an impromptu crafting session. They made decorations from popcorn and cranberries while her mom shared stories about her own childhood Christmases in Mexico.

"Though maybe we shouldn't recreate the time I tried to fill piñatas with hot chocolate," her mom laughed. "That was... festively messy."

The snow globe sparkled, showing young Mom covered in cocoa powder, creating a Christmas chaos that made Olivia's plans look amateur.

Even her ultimate scheme—scheduling three different church choir performances that overlapped—backfired beautifully. Instead of stress, she ended up with both parents sitting together at the last performance, both wearing light-up Christmas accessories (Dad's tie had competition from Mom's flashing poinsettia brooch), both cheering embarrassingly loud when she sang.

The snow globe really outdid itself that evening, floating between memories of both her parents performing in their own childhood choir concerts, showing how music had always been a part of their family story.

"You know," her dad said after the concert, his tie playing a jazzy version of 'Silent Night,' "just because things are different doesn't mean they can't be twice as special."

Her mom nodded, her brooch twinkling. "Though maybe we could coordinate our musical accessories next time. We're clashing in at least three Christmas songs."

Olivia looked between them, realizing something important. The snow globe wasn't just showing her their past—it was helping her see how to build their future. Different houses didn't mean different hearts. And maybe, just maybe, two Christmases meant twice the magic.

That night, in her room at Dad's house, Olivia pulled out her journal and started a list:

New Holiday Traditions for Our Two-House Adventure.
1. Dad's infamous Christmas tie must make an appearance at both celebrations (but only for maximum 10 minutes per house—there's only so much electronic Rudolph anyone can take)
2. Mom's stress-baking gets distributed equally (especially the triple chocolate peppermint cookies)

3. Annual competition for Most Embarrassing Holiday Accessory (current champion: Dad's singing socks)
4. Two different trees = twice the hiding spots for presents!
5. Both houses must maintain minimum dad-joke quotient (even Mom's house—rules are rules)

The snow globe on her nightstand glowed softly, and in its depths, she saw new memories being made—future Christmases full of laughter, love, and yes, even those terrible musical accessories...

Christmas Eve arrived with a flurry of activity and the distinct possibility that Dad's tie had learned a new song—though it sounded suspiciously like "Jingle Bells" having a melodic identity crisis.

Olivia had her schedule down pat: Christmas Eve dinner at Dad's, midnight hot chocolate at Mom's, Christmas morning presents at Mom's, Christmas dinner at Dad's, and somehow, magically, no stress about any of it. The snow globe had shown her enough memories to realize that holiday chaos was actually a long-standing family tradition.

At Dad's house, the kitchen looked like a Christmas tornado had hit a flour factory. He was attempting to recreate Abuela's tamales recipe while FaceTiming with Mom for instructions.

"No, Miguel, the masa shouldn't be that... liquidy," Mom was saying, trying not to laugh. "It's supposed to float in water, not become the water."

"I'm innovating!" Dad protested, wearing what appeared to be half the masa as an accidental facial mask. "Besides, remember your Great Hot Chocolate Disaster of '95?"

The snow globe, sitting on the counter (and somehow staying remarkably clean despite the cooking chaos), swirled to show teenage Mom creating what looked like a chocolate volcano in her parents' kitchen.

"That's it!" Olivia announced, hitting the FaceTime button. "Mom, come over. We're having a Christmas Eve Cooking Challenge!"

And somehow, it worked. Within an hour, Mom arrived with her own recipe box and a new light-up Christmas apron that played "Feliz Navidad" when you pressed the Rudolph nose. Between Dad's enthusiastic but misguided attempts at tamales and Mom's determination to finally master her grandmother's pozole recipe, the kitchen became command central for what they dubbed *The Great Holiday Food Festival.*

The snow globe kept showing glimpses of past family celebrations, but now Olivia noticed something new—the memories were mixing together, creating a beautiful blend of traditions from both sides of her family.

"You know what this needs?" Dad asked, his tie now performing a duet with Mom's apron. "Background music!"

Before anyone could stop him, he pulled out his phone and started playing his infamous Christmas playlist—the one that mixed traditional carols with pop covers and, for some inexplicable reason, disco versions of holiday classics.

"Oh no," Mom groaned, but she was already swaying to the beat. "Not the Funky Santa Mix."

"Oh yes," Dad grinned, offering his hand. "May I have this dance, Chef Martinez?"

And there, in the masa-covered kitchen, with "Disco Deck the Halls" playing in the background, Olivia watched her parents dance and laugh like they used to, but somehow better—because now it wasn't about being perfect, it was about being real.

The snow globe glowed brighter than ever, and in its depths, Olivia saw something remarkable: future Christmases, full of merged traditions and new ones they hadn't even invented yet. Two houses, two celebrations, but one family—just with a little more room to grow.

"I think," she announced, as her parents attempted to twirl without knocking over the salsa, "we need to make the *Christmas Eve Cooking Challenge* an official tradition. But maybe with less masa on the ceiling next year?"

"Seconded!" Mom laughed, wiping flour from Dad's nose.

"Motion carried!" Dad declared, his tie celebrating with a slightly off-key rendition of "We Wish You a Merry Christmas."

Later that night, as Olivia packed her bag for the short trip to Mom's house for midnight hot chocolate, she looked at her list of new traditions and smiled. At the bottom, she added one more:

6. Remember that love doesn't divide when you multiply it by two—it just grows bigger, messier, and way more fun.

The snow globe twinkled in agreement, and somewhere in the background, Dad's tie started playing "Auld Lang Syne"—three days early, but somehow perfectly timed.

Because sometimes the best Christmas magic isn't about keeping things the same—it's about discovering that change can bring twice the joy, twice the laughter, and definitely twice the questionable musical accessories.

Christmas morning dawned with a dusting of fresh snow and the now-familiar journey between houses. But this year, instead of feeling split between two worlds, Olivia felt like she had a Christmas story being written in stereo.

At Mom's house, they opened presents in their matching holiday pajamas (a tradition Dad had insisted they keep, even ordering an extra set for Mom). Through the snow globe, Olivia watched both her parents' childhood Christmas mornings blend together—her dad's family opening gifts at dawn, her mom's waiting until after breakfast. Now they had time for both.

Her phone buzzed with a text from Dad: "Check the bottom of your stocking!"

Inside was a small wrapped package with two cards. One read "From Dad" and the other "From Mom"—they'd actually coordinated presents this year. Inside was a delicate charm bracelet, with each parent contributing different charms: a tiny piano from Mom for her music, a miniature book from Dad for her stories, and in the middle, a perfect little snow globe charm they'd picked out together.

The real snow globe glowed warmly, showing her parents shopping separately but choosing pieces that fit together perfectly—just like their new way of being a family.

"Your father always did have good taste in jewelry," Mom said softly, helping Olivia fasten the bracelet. There was no sadness in her voice, just warm remembrance and appreciation.

Later, during Christmas dinner at Dad's, Mom stopped by to drop off more cookies ("Because your father still can't bake to save his life," she teased). Instead of awkward tension, they all ended up in the living room, sharing stories about past Christmases while Dad's tie and Mom's brooch performed an unintentional holiday concert.

"Remember our first Christmas tree?" Dad asked Mom, grinning. "When we tried to fit that twelve-foot monster into our tiny apartment?"

"And it fell over three times!" Mom laughed. "The neighbors below us thought we were having earthquakes!"

The snow globe swirled with that memory—young Mom and Dad, surrounded by fallen ornaments, laughing until they cried. But now Olivia understood: just because a story has a different ending doesn't make the middle chapters any less precious.

They weren't a broken family; they were just a family that had learned how to love bigger, beyond the boundaries of a single home. And maybe that was the real Christmas magic—not the perfect holiday card moment, but the messy, wonderful reality of people who chose to keep caring, keep trying, and keep celebrating together, just in a new way.

Besides, as Dad pointed out while serving his slightly crushed but still delicious Christmas pie, "Now you get twice the holiday desserts, Liv. If that's not a Christmas miracle, I don't know what is!"

The snow globe twinkled one last time, showing not past or future, but this exact moment: a family laughing together, different but whole, proving that love doesn't need one address to call home.

It just needs heart. And maybe a few musical accessories.

CHAPTER 6
The Exchange Student's First Christmas

"So, the tree goes inside the house?" Mei Lin asked, watching Sarah's dad wrestle with an enormous pine through their front door. "And you... decorate it? Like a very large houseplant?"

Sarah Bennett tried not to laugh at her exchange student's bewildered expression. "Pretty much. Though most houseplants don't come with built-in squirrels."

As if on cue, a tiny grey head poked out from the branches, looked around indignantly, and scampered back into the tree.

"Dad!" Sarah called out. "I think this one came with bonus wildlife!"

"Well, that's the last time I let your mother talk me into getting a tree from *Discount Dave's Premium Pines and Pizza*." Her dad muttered, attempting to shake the squirrel out while keeping his Santa hat from falling off. "Though I have to admit, the buy-one-get-one-free pizza deal was pretty good."

Mei watched the chaos unfold with fascination. She'd been living with the Bennetts for three months now, but American holiday traditions still surprised her daily. Last week, she'd discovered eggnog ("Like drinking melted ice cream, but... spicier?") and yesterday, she'd learned about ugly Christmas sweater competitions ("But why make clothing intentionally ugly?").

The kitchen timer chimed, and a wonderful aroma wafted through the house. Sarah's mom was attempting to recreate Mei's favorite spice cookies from home, while simultaneously teaching herself how to say "Merry Christmas" in Mandarin through a rather questionable translation app.

"Shèngdàn kuàilè!" Mrs. Bennett called out proudly from the kitchen, though it came out sounding more like "Singing ducks are late!"

Mei giggled, then immediately felt a pang of homesickness. Her own mother would be preparing for the Lunar New Year now, their small apartment filled with the scent of star anise and ginger.

As if reading her thoughts, something magical happened. The spices from Mrs. Bennett's baking seemed to shift and swirl in the air, creating invisible patterns that only Mei could see. The scent of cinnamon transformed into the familiar aroma of her mother's five-spice blend, then back again, like two songs harmonizing.

"Oh!" Sarah exclaimed suddenly. "Mom's trying your cookie recipe, but we could make my grandmother's gingerbread too! Double the cookies, double the fun!"

The spice-magic swirled stronger, and Mei felt her homesickness fade slightly. "Could I... could I show you how my mom makes eight-treasure rice too? It's not exactly Christmas food, but—"

"Are you kidding? It has 'treasure' in the name! That's totally Christmas!" Sarah's enthusiasm was infectious. "Besides, Mom always says holiday traditions are just different families' ways of showing love through food."

"Speaking of family traditions," Mr. Bennett interrupted, still battling the tree, "could someone please help me convince our new squirrel friend that pinecones are not actually Christmas ornaments?"

The girls rushed to help, but not before the squirrel had arranged several pinecones in what was, they had to admit, a rather artistic pattern on the lower branches.

"Well," Sarah's mom emerged from the kitchen, covered in flour and holding a plate of slightly lopsided but wonderful-smelling cookies, "I guess we have our first new tradition of the year: squirrel-decorated Christmas trees!"

The magical spice aromas danced again, and Mei realized something—maybe feeling like an outsider wasn't about being foreign or different. Maybe it was just part of finding your place, like a new spice finding its way into a familiar recipe.

The kitchen quickly became command central for what Sarah dubbed *The Great Holiday Fusion Experiment*. Every surface was covered with ingredients from both cultures, and the magical spices kept creating bridges between them.

"So gingerbread is like mooncakes?" Mei asked, watching Sarah attempt to roll out dough. "Special treats that tell stories?"

"Exactly! Though I don't think mooncakes usually look like slightly squashed reindeer," Sarah laughed, holding up her questionable creation. "This one looks more like a deer having a very rough day."

The cinnamon in the air swirled playfully, mixing with the star anise Mei was using, creating tiny sparkles only they could see. Each spice seemed to carry memories: Sarah's grandmother teaching her the perfect gingerbread ratio, Mei's mother showing her how to blend the perfect five-spice powder.

"You know what's weird?" Sarah said, decorating her misshapen reindeer with perhaps too many candies. "I always feel kind of different during Christmas too. Like, everyone else seems to know exactly what they're doing, and I'm just here making mutant cookie animals."

Mei nodded, understanding completely. "In China, I was too interested in Western things. Here, I worry about being too Chinese. It's like... like..."

"Like being a squirrel in a Christmas tree?" Sarah suggested, pointing to their new friend who had returned to rearrange the pinecones.

"We named him Nutcracker, by the way," Mr. Bennett announced, passing through the kitchen with more decorations. "He's appointed himself Chief Ornament Supervisor."

The spice-magic sparkled with approval, and suddenly both girls were laughing, the tension of being "different" dissolving like sugar cookies in hot chocolate.

They spent the afternoon creating what they called "fusion festivities." Mei taught Sarah's mom the proper way to fold dumplings ("No, Mrs. Bennett, they shouldn't look like tiny boxing gloves!"), while Sarah introduced Mei to the art of building a gingerbread house, which quickly turned into a gingerbread pagoda complete with candy cane columns.

The magical spices seemed to delight in their experiments, creating swirling patterns that connected every new tradition they invented. When Mei sprinkled five-spice powder on the sugar cookies, the aroma danced with the vanilla extract, creating a scent that somehow reminded both girls of home.

"Hey," Sarah said suddenly, "want to see something cool?" She led Mei to the living room closet and pulled out a box labeled 'Special Occasions Only (This Means You, Dad)'. Inside was a collection of glass ornaments, each filled with different spices and dried fruits.

"My great-grandmother started this," Sarah explained. "Every year, each family member adds a new one with their favorite scents. Mom says it's like capturing memories in glass."

The spice-magic surged, and Mei gasped as each ornament began to glow softly, releasing tiny wisps of fragrance that told stories: citrus and clove from holidays long past, cinnamon and apple from recent celebrations, each one a precious memory preserved.

"Would you... would you like to make one?" Sarah asked shyly. "I mean, you're family now, even if it's just for this year."

Mei felt tears prick her eyes, but they were happy tears. "Could we make one with star anise and orange? Like the tea my grandmother always makes?"

That evening, as they hung their new ornament on the tree (under Nutcracker's careful supervision), something wonderful happened. All the spice-magic gathered together, creating a warm glow that wrapped around them like a hug. The scents of both their homes, both their families, both their traditions swirled together in perfect harmony.

Mrs. Bennett appeared with hot chocolate topped with both marshmallows and the sweet red beans Mei loved. Mr. Bennett wore his Santa hat at what he called a "culturally inclusive angle." And Nutcracker had somehow managed to arrange his pinecones in a pattern that looked suspiciously like Chinese characters.

"You know what this means?" Sarah grinned. "Next year, we're definitely doing a Chinese New Year tree. With red envelopes for everyone!"

"Even Nutcracker?" Mei asked, watching their squirrel friend attempt to hang a candy cane.

"Especially Nutcracker. He's family now too."

The spice-magic twinkled in agreement, reminding them that the best traditions aren't the ones you're born into, but the ones you create together. And sometimes, the most wonderful holiday moments happen when different kinds of magic—whether it's Christmas lights or lucky red envelopes, gingerbread or eight-treasure rice, or even spice-induced enchantment—find a way to dance together in perfect harmony.

Besides, as Mr. Bennett pointed out while attempting to prevent Nutcracker from adding more "decorations" to the tree, any holiday that ends with double the desserts and a squirrel wearing a tiny paper Santa hat is definitely a tradition worth keeping.

CHAPTER 7
Gingerbread Legacy

Isabella Morgan stood in her family's bakery, *Morgans' Sweet Memories*, surrounded by the chaos of packing boxes and the lingering scent of vanilla. Her phone was propped against a mixing bowl, open to yet another perfect #ChristmasBaking post that made her stomach twist with anxiety.

She'd spent years watching her mother and grandmother create magic in this kitchen, sitting on the counter since she was little, dusted in flour, and learning family secrets. But lately, she'd started sitting further away from the mixing bowls, declining taste tests, trying to become smaller in a world that seemed to demand perfection.

Middle school had changed things. Suddenly, the comfort she'd always found in baking became complicated by lunch table comments and social media posts about clean eating and calories. The haven of her family's bakery felt at odds with a world of filters and "What I Eat in a Day" videos.

"Nobody wants old-fashioned cookies anymore," she muttered, looking at the empty display cases that had once held her grandmother's famous treats. "They want things that look good on social media, made by people who look good on social media."

She touched the worn counter where her height had been marked in pencil over the years, each line paired with a special treat: "Isabella, age 6—first solo chocolate chip cookies (mostly edible)" and "Isabella, age 9—mastered snickerdoodles (only two burned)." The last mark was from over a year ago, before she'd started declining Gran's baking lessons.

A loud crash from the kItchen interrupted her train of thought. "Gran's reorganizing again!" her mother called out. "Bella, could you...?"

Isabella hurried to the back, where her grandmother was pulling ancient baking sheets from the highest shelves, humming "Jingle Bells" slightly off-key. The sight of Gran in her flour-dusted apron, wearing the reading glasses she'd decorated with sparkly candy canes, brought back memories of easier days.

Days before Gran started forgetting things, before the bakery started struggling, before Isabella started worrying about fitting into a world that seemed to have such strict rules about how to look and be.

"We need to find it," Gran announced, reaching for another shelf. "The blue book with the star on it. Christmas isn't Christmas without Morgan magic!"

"Gran, careful!" Isabella caught a falling rolling pin. "What blue book?"

"The one with all the secrets, silly girl! Your great-great-grandmother started it. She knew that sometimes people need more than just cookies—they need memories baked with love!"

Before Isabella could respond, a dusty volume tumbled from the top shelf, landing with a soft thump. It was bound in faded blue leather, with a tarnished silver star on its cover. As Isabella picked it up, the strangest thing happened—the star seemed to warm under her fingers, and the scent of freshly baked gingerbread filled the air.

"See?" Gran smiled knowingly. "Magic!"

Isabella opened the book carefully. Inside were handwritten recipes, notes scribbled in margins, and photos of Morgan women through the generations. As she touched the first page, something extraordinary happened. The recipe for "Victory Gingerbread" began to glow softly, and suddenly she could see the memory it held...

Her great-great-grandmother Sarah Morgan stood in this very kitchen during World War II, when sugar was rationed and butter was scarce. But instead of giving up, she'd created a recipe using molasses and applesauce, proving that sweetness could be found even in hard times.

"That's my mother's writing," Gran said clearly, having one of her lucid moments. "She always said the secret ingredient was determination. Also nutmeg, but mostly determination."

Isabella turned the page, and another memory shimmered to life. Her grandmother as a teenager, creating rainbow cookies for the first Pride parade in their small town, proving that love came in all colors and deserved to be celebrated.

"I was scared," Gran admitted, touching the page gently. "But cookies have a way of bringing people together. Besides," she winked, "it's hard to be angry while eating something delicious."

The book seemed to pulse with magic, and Isabella realized something—every recipe told a story of a Morgan woman facing a challenge. None of them had been perfect, but all of them had been brave.

"Hey, Gran?" Isabella pulled out her phone with sudden inspiration. "Want to teach me how to make your famous gingerbread? But maybe... maybe we could add our own twist?"

Gran's eyes lit up with recognition. "First, we need the right music," she declared, turning on the ancient radio that had survived decades of flour dustings. As Bing Crosby crooned about white Christmases, the magical cookbook seemed to hum along.

Isabella set up her phone camera while Gran gathered ingredients, moving with surprising certainty. "The secret," Gran explained, "is to dance while you measure. Happy feet make happy sweets!"

As they worked, more memories sprang from the cookbook's pages. Isabella saw her mother winning a baking competition with chocolate chip cookies during the 1990s—except the chips had melted in the summer heat. Instead of panicking, she'd swirled the melted chocolate through the dough, accidentally inventing their famous marble cookies.

"That's it!" Isabella exclaimed. "We don't have to choose between old and new. We just have to blend them together!"

She started filming as Gran demonstrated the perfect gingerbread technique, adding her own modern twists. They sprinkled matcha powder over some cookies, added orange zest to others, and created a whole batch with tiny candied ginger pieces that Gran swore would "wake up your taste buds and make them dance the cha-cha."

The cookbook's pages glowed brighter with each innovation, as if approving their experiments. When Isabella accidentally dropped too much cinnamon in the dough, the book fluttered to a page showing her great-aunt Mary's "Happy Accident Snickerdoodles" from 1962.

"Mistakes?" Gran chuckled, reading her mind. "Oh, honey, some of our best recipes started as mistakes. Did I ever tell you about the time I put salt instead of sugar in the Christmas cookies? Your grandfather ate them all anyway, said they were perfect for his low-sugar diet!"

As they baked, Isabella found herself relaxing in front of the camera, sharing family stories and baking tips. She didn't even mind when flour dusted her shirt or when Gran insisted they wear the sparkly antique aprons that had belonged to four generations of Morgan women.

"Your great-grandmother wore this one when she baked cookies for the hospital during the flu epidemic," Gran said, straightening Isabella's apron. "She said spotted aprons meant spotted cookies, but spotted cookies meant happy patients."

✧

Isabella posted their baking video that evening, adding the hashtag #MorganMagicMemories. By morning, it had hundreds of views.

Comments poured in about how refreshing it was to see real people baking real food, making real mistakes, and having real fun.

"Look, Gran!" Isabella showed her the phone. "They love your dance-while-you-bake technique!"

The magical cookbook chose that moment to reveal another memory: Gran as a young woman, dancing in the kitchen while very pregnant with Isabella's mother, declaring that "babies baked with joy come out extra sweet!"

More videos followed. Isabella and Gran made "Memory Lane Macarons" with traditional fillings and modern flavors. They created "Heritage Honey Cakes" using Gran's mother's recipe but decorated them with edible flowers for a contemporary touch.

The bakery's Instagram following grew, but more importantly, so did the line outside their door. People came for the treats they saw online but stayed for the stories Gran told, even on her confused days. Something about her mixing up decades and recipes made everyone feel at home with their own imperfections.

One afternoon, while making "Courage Cookies" (a recipe Isabella's great-grandmother had created during the Depression), Gran had a moment of perfect clarity.

"You know what all these recipes really are?" she asked, pointing to the glowing cookbook. "They're love letters. To our families, to our customers, to ourselves. Even when times change, even when memories fade, love stays. It just takes different shapes. Like cookies!"

Isabella looked at their latest creation—classic gingerbread decorated with metallic edible paint, traditional shapes with modern flair. Just like her: a blend of past and present, of Morgan magic and her own style.

The cookbook's star pulsed warmly, and Isabella realized she hadn't checked a social media filter all day. She'd been too busy living her own story, adding her chapter to the Morgan legacy.

"Hey Gran," she said, reaching for more ginger, "want to invent a new tradition?"

Gran's eyes twinkled. "As long as it involves dancing!"

And so, surrounded by the scent of spices and the sound of old Christmas songs, a grandmother who sometimes forgot and a granddaughter who was learning to remember created something completely new: cookies that tasted like heritage and hope, decorated with both wisdom and wonder.

After all, as the magical cookbook seemed to whisper through its glowing pages, the sweetest memories are the ones we bake together, imperfections and all.

On Christmas Eve, Isabella made one final video. This time, she faced the camera directly, flour on her cheek and pride in her smile.

"Today, we're making what we call 'Perfectly Imperfect Christmas Cookies,'" she announced, as Gran danced through the background with a mixing bowl. "And I want to tell you a story about something my grandmother taught me."

The magical cookbook glowed warmly as Isabella continued, "For a while, I thought I had to be perfect to be worthy of our family's baking legacy. I stopped tasting the cookies I made. I worried more about how things looked than how they felt. But here's what I learned from this magical old book and my even more magical grandmother..."

She held up two gingerbread cookies—one perfectly shaped and decorated, the other slightly wonky but covered in colorful, creative icing. "This perfect cookie? It's beautiful, but it doesn't tell a story. But this one?" She showed the imperfect cookie. "This one shows where my hand shook while piping the icing because I was laughing at Gran's jokes. The uneven edge is from where I got distracted telling stories about my mom's baking adventures. Every 'flaw' is actually a moment of joy."

Behind her, the cookbook's pages rustled by themselves, showing generations of Morgan women who had each discovered their own way of being enough.

"So this Christmas," Isabella smiled, "Morgans' Sweet Memories isn't closing. We're evolving. We're going to keep baking the old recipes and creating new ones. We're going to celebrate perfectly imperfect moments. And most importantly," she winked at Gran, who was now attempting to teach her mother the 'happiness hop' while measuring flour, "we're going to keep dancing while we bake!"

The video ended up being their most shared post ever, but that wasn't the real victory. The real triumph was in the new height mark added to the counter: "Isabella, age 13—mastered being herself (perfectly imperfect)."

That night, as they closed the bakery, the magical cookbook had one final memory to share. It showed Isabella herself, from just that morning, laughing and tasting cookie dough, her face bright with joy rather than worry. The image glowed with the same warmth as all the other cherished memories in its pages.

"Well, look at that," Gran said clearly, patting Isabella's hand. "You're part of the magic now too."

Isabella hugged her grandmother, both of them smelling of gingerbread and happiness. Outside, snow began to fall, and the bakery's old sign flickered to life: *Morgans' Sweet Memories—Where Every Batch is Baked with Love.*

And for the first time in a long while, Isabella knew that love included loving herself, measuring cups of self-acceptance along with the sugar and flour.

After all, as five generations of Morgan women had proved, the sweetest legacy isn't perfection—it's the courage to be authentically, wonderfully, deliciously yourself.

CHAPTER 8
The 12 Days of Friendship

Grace Chen stared at her locker, which someone had "helpfully" decorated with a slightly deranged-looking paper snowman. Its crooked smile and googly eyes (three of them, because apparently this snowman had seen things) perfectly summed up her current social situation—trying to look happy while feeling decidedly off-kilter.

"Well, at least you're having a weird December too," she told the snowman, whose third eye wobbled sympathetically as she spun her combination lock.

Three months since *The Great Lunch Table Divide* (as everyone now dramatically called it), and the school cafeteria had turned into a carefully mapped war zone. The former friend group had split into two tables—Olivia, Madison, and Kiera claimed their usual spot by the window, while Grace sat with Jamie and Sophie near the vending machine that occasionally ate people's lunch money and played "Jingle Bells" as compensation.

"It's fine," Grace muttered, opening her locker. "Totally fine. Everything is fine."

She froze. There, sitting on top of her chemistry textbook, was a small gift wrapped in silver paper with tiny snowflakes. A tag read: "On the first day of Christmas, your true friend gives to thee…"

"If this is some weird Pinterest-inspired secret admirer thing," Grace grumbled, "I'm moving to the North Pole to live with the elves." But she opened it anyway.

Inside was a friendship bracelet—exactly like the ones they'd all made at summer camp last year. As soon as she touched it, something magical happened. The bracelet glowed softly, and suddenly she could see two memories at once.

In one, she was laughing with Olivia while they tangled embroidery threads and sang off-key camp songs. In the other, she saw what she'd missed: Olivia staying up late to remake her bracelet after the first one fell apart, wanting it to be perfect for her best friend.

"Okay, that was weird," Grace whispered, blinking away the vision. The three-eyed snowman seemed to wink at her. Or maybe it was just losing another googly eye.

The warning bell rang, sending students scurrying like startled reindeer. Grace slipped the bracelet into her pocket, trying not to think about how Olivia still wore hers every day.

In history class, she found herself sitting behind Kiera for the first time since September. The awkward silence was broken only by their teacher's enthusiastic explanation of medieval Christmas traditions, which apparently involved a lot more wild boars and questionable singing than modern celebrations.

"And they would gather in great halls," Mr. Patterson announced, "to share the wassail bowl! Which was not, as Miss Rodriguez suggested last period, medieval Red Bull."

Grace caught Kiera stifling a laugh and almost smiled herself before remembering they weren't doing that anymore. The friendship bracelet in her pocket seemed to warm slightly, as if saying "Oh, really?"

When she got home that afternoon, she found herself digging through her memory box, pulling out photos and notes from happier times. The bracelet glowed again, showing more double-sided memories: the time she and Madison had gotten lost during the Halloween corn maze and turned it into an adventure; the day Jamie had helped her with math while she was struggling, even though they weren't close friends yet.

"But how do you fix something when everyone's a little bit right and a little bit wrong?" she asked her bedroom ceiling. "And when did I start talking to inanimate objects so much?"

Her phone buzzed with a text from Sophie about tomorrow's Christmas choir practice, which would definitely not be awkward at all, considering half the friend group was in soprano section and half in alto. They'd been avoiding harmonizing for months.

Grace flopped onto her bed, still holding the magical bracelet. "I wish..."

But before she could finish that thought, she noticed something new appearing in her backpack—another small gift, this one wrapped in gold paper.

The three-eyed snowman drawing had somehow migrated from her locker to her notebook, and now it was holding a tiny sign that read: "On the second day of Christmas..."

Grace reached for the second gift, half expecting it to burst into festive glitter. Inside was a small snow globe featuring a miniature school cafeteria. "Oh great," she muttered. "Even holiday decorations are mocking me now."

But when she shook it, instead of snow, memories swirled inside. She saw Madison stress-eating her way through three pudding cups after bombing a math test, while simultaneously offering her last cookie to a crying freshman. She saw Kiera pretending not to be hurt when no one noticed her new haircut. She saw herself, head buried in her phone, missing moments when others had tried to reach out.

"Okay, mysterious gift-giver," Grace sighed, "I get it. We all have our stories. But that doesn't—"

Her phone buzzed with a choir reminder: "MANDATORY Christmas Concert Practice Tomorrow! Attendance = 40% of Grade (Yes, we're serious. No, Mr. Harrison's ugly Christmas sweater will not distract us from taking attendance this year)."

Grace groaned. Tomorrow she'd have to stand between Olivia and Madison for two hours, pretending not to notice how they were both deliberately singing slightly off-key to avoid harmonizing with each other. Last week's practice had turned "Silent Night" into "Passive-Aggressive Night."

The next morning, a third gift waited in her locker: a packet of hot chocolate mix with tiny marshmallows shaped like musical notes. The moment she picked it up, another double memory played:

Last year's Christmas concert, when they'd all shared a thermos of hot chocolate behind the risers, trying not to giggle during the solemn parts. But now she also saw how Sophie, who hadn't been part of their group then, had watched longingly from across the room, wishing she had someone to laugh with.

"We weren't always nice, were we?" Grace whispered to the three-eyed snowman, which had now acquired a tiny Santa hat and what appeared to be jazz hands.

During practice, something odd happened. When they reached "Joy to the World," Grace noticed Olivia actually singing her part properly. Their voices blended for a moment, and it felt... okay. Different from before, but not bad.

The fourth gift appeared during lunch: a friendship bracelet repair kit. The memory this time showed all the times they'd fixed each other's bracelets throughout the year, but also the moments when they'd ignored bigger things that needed fixing.

Days five through eight brought more revelations: A shared pencil case revealed times of both generosity and pettiness. A pack of Christmas stickers showed moments of inclusion and exclusion. A mini photo album displayed happy memories alongside missed opportunities for kindness.

By day nine, Grace had started to understand. The gifts weren't about erasing the past or forcing a perfect reunion. They were about seeing the whole picture—the good, the messy, and the complicated in-between.

The tenth gift was a small mirror that showed reflections of how others saw you. Grace spent an hour watching scenes play out: times she'd been a good friend, times she hadn't, times she'd tried her best but still got it wrong.

"It's not about being perfect," she realized. "It's about being real."

On day eleven, she found a Christmas card with everyone's signatures—not just her old friends, but Sophie and Jamie too. But these signatures moved, showing each person writing with hesitation, hope, and hints of both regret and forgiveness.

The final gift appeared on the last day before winter break. It was a new friendship bracelet, but this one was different—woven with threads from all their old bracelets plus some new ones, creating a pattern that was both familiar and fresh.

At lunch that day, Grace did something brave. She moved her seat to the neutral territory between the two tables. After a moment, Sophie joined her. Then Jamie. Then, slowly, the others drifted over.

It was awkward, and the groups didn't blend together perfectly anymore, but they talked across the space, sharing Christmas cookies and cautious smiles. It wasn't perfect harmony, but it was something new—something real.

"So," Madison said carefully, "anyone going to the winter carnival this weekend?"

"I heard they have a three-eyed snowman display," Grace found herself saying. "Apparently it does jazz hands."

The surprise of shared laughter felt like the best gift of all.

That afternoon, Grace found one last note in her locker. It read: "Sometimes the best friendships aren't the ones that stay the same, but the ones that grow enough to let everyone change."

The three-eyed snowman drawing had acquired a graduation cap and appeared to be crying glitter tears of joy.

Below it, twelve signatures—old friends and new—had written: "Here's to growing together, even if we're growing differently. Merry Christmas!"

Grace touched her new bracelet, feeling its warmth. Sometimes the best Christmas magic isn't about fixing what's broken, but about finding beauty in the way things rebuild themselves into something new.

Even if that something new occasionally involves three-eyed snowmen with jazz hands.

SECTION 3: SANTA'S HELPERS

Sleigh bells ring, pine needles scatter, and somewhere in the distance, a retirement home tinsel does a celebratory dance...

What's that twinkle in the air? That shimmer of possibility? That feeling that something wonderfully festive is about to unfold? Why, it's the unmistakable sign that you're about to meet Santa's most extraordinary helpers!

But don't expect pointy ears and striped stockings here! These helpers come with homework planners, anxiety-induced butterflies, volunteer badges, and hearts bigger than Santa's gift bag. They're the ones who prove that Christmas magic doesn't need flying reindeer—sometimes it just needs someone brave enough to let it shine.

Prepare to be enchanted by:
Talking Christmas trees with a PhD in life lessons
Retirement home decorations with impeccable timing
Glitter trails that lead to community miracles
And a holiday market booth that knows exactly who needs to find it

We've got disco-dancing reindeer, sweaters that sing on command, fairy lights with distinct personalities, and enough Christmas spirit to make even the grumpiest decorator crack a smile.

Grab another cozy blanket to add to the others, re-pour your hot chocolate (extra, extra, marshmallows recommended), and settle in for tales that remind us that Santa's helpers come in all forms. Some may struggle with reading, others with talking, and a few might be new in town—but they all share one magical quality: the ability to see what needs to be done and the courage to do it.

A wise Christmas tree once whispered (yes, really):
"The best kind of holiday helper isn't the one with the fanciest sleigh... It's the one who makes others believe in magic again."

Now, who's ready to discover some seriously spectacular Christmas spirit?

Cue the twinkling lights, a sprinkle of magical glitter, and perhaps a sneaky piece of tinsel spelling out "Welcome!"

Let the enchantment begin!

CHAPTER 9
The Christmas Tree Lot Teacher

Zoe Collins's to-do list was longer than a string of Christmas lights, and about as tangled. Between AP classes, debate team captain duties, volunteer hours, and her family's Christmas tree lot, she was running on candy canes and determination.

"And now they want me to tutor?" she muttered, stapling yet another price tag to yet another Fraser fir. "Because apparently sleep is optional in December?"

The tree shivered slightly, though there wasn't any wind. Zoe blamed it on caffeine-induced hallucinations. That's what happens when you replace breakfast with peppermint lattes five days in a row.

"Talking to the trees again, sweetie?" Her dad appeared, wearing his signature red plaid jacket and a Santa hat that had seen better decades. "They're good listeners. Better than your brother when it's his turn to sweep up pine needles."

"I'm fine, Dad. Just... optimizing my schedule." Zoe checked her color-coded planner, which now had more highlights than actual white space. "If I tutor during tree lot shifts, I can still maintain my GPA, finish my college essays, and maybe even remember to eat lunch occasionally."

The tree shivered again, this time definitely dropping a pine needle in judgment.

"Ah, yes," her dad nodded sagely. "Because nothing says 'Christmas spirit' like multitasking yourself into a candy cane-colored stress spiral."

Before Zoe could protest that stress spirals were totally part of her efficiency strategy, a boy about her age trudged into the lot. He wore a letterman jacket from her high school and an expression that suggested he'd rather be anywhere else.

"You must be Ryan," her dad said cheerfully. "The one who needs help with chemistry?"

"The one who's being forced to care about chemistry," Ryan corrected, shooting a look at the textbook under his arm like it had personally offended him.

Great. A reluctant student. Just what her perfectly planned schedule needed.

But then something weird happened. The massive Blue Spruce behind Ryan seemed to stretch its branches, creating a perfect study nook complete with a bench-like root structure. The surrounding trees leaned in slightly, forming walls that blocked the December wind.

"Did those trees just... move?" Ryan asked.

"Climate change," Zoe said quickly. "Very concerning. Let's talk about electron configurations."

As she pulled out her own textbook (color-coded tabs perfectly aligned, obviously), she could have sworn she heard the trees whispering. Something about "growth" and "patience" and "girl, you need to chill."

But that was ridiculous. Trees didn't whisper....did they?

The first tutoring session went exactly as Zoe expected—which is to say, not according to her meticulously planned study guide at all. Ryan kept getting distracted by customers selecting trees, and Zoe's perfectly structured atomic theory explanation was repeatedly interrupted by the Blue Spruce dropping pinecones whenever she started talking too fast.

"Okay," she sighed after the fifth pinecone bombardment, "maybe we should try something different."

"Like admitting chemistry is pointless?" Ryan suggested hopefully.

The trees rustled disapprovingly. A small Douglas fir actually wagged its top branch like a disappointed teacher.

"No," Zoe said, suddenly inspired. "Like... using the trees to explain molecular bonds. See how they all support each other? Kind of like atoms sharing electrons."

To her surprise, Ryan sat up straighter. "So, like how this big guy," he patted the Blue Spruce, "needs all these smaller trees around it to block the wind?"

The Blue Spruce preened noticeably.

"Exactly!" Zoe found herself getting excited. "And look at how the branches grow—they're following patterns, just like electron shells!"

As they talked, Zoe noticed something strange. The more she relaxed her grip on her perfect lesson plan, the more the trees seemed to help. They created object lessons by dropping perfectly shaped pinecones to represent atomic structures. They shifted their branches to demonstrate different types of bonds. One young Fraser fir even managed to spell out "COVALENT" with its shadows (though its spelling was admittedly questionable).

Between customers, Zoe and Ryan developed their own strange rhythm. They'd work on chemistry while wrapping trees in netting, practice formulas while sweeping up needles, and use garland to model molecular chains. Ryan turned out to have a knack for remembering concepts when they were explained through Christmas metaphors.

"So ionic bonds are like secret Santa," he said one day, helping her adjust a tree in its stand. "One atom gives electrons, one receives them, everyone's happy?"

"That's... actually a really good way to think about it," Zoe admitted, surprised.

The trees swayed approvingly, and she could have sworn she heard them humming "Chemistry Boy" to the tune of "Jingle Bells."

But it wasn't just Ryan who was learning. Every day, the trees seemed to whisper new wisdom: about how the tallest pines took decades to grow, about how even crooked branches found their place in the forest, about how growth couldn't be rushed or perfectly planned.

That Saturday, everything finally reached its tipping point. Zoe was balancing her phone between her shoulder and ear (talking to the debate team about their holiday fundraiser) while simultaneously trying to explain ionic bonds to Ryan and ring up a sale for a young couple who couldn't decide between a Balsam or Fraser fir. Her coffee had gone cold hours ago, her stomach was growling loud enough to startle the chickadees in the trees, and she'd just noticed a massive typo in her college essay draft.

That's when the *Great Tree Intervention* occurred.

It started with the Blue Spruce—a soft whisper of movement, like someone taking a deep breath. Then the Douglas firs joined in, their branches swaying in a non-existent breeze. The motion spread through the lot like a wave: Norway Spruces, Noble Firs, even the little Charlie Brown tree in the corner that nobody wanted to buy.

"Um, Zoe?" Ryan pointed upward. "Is this normal?"

Every single tree in the lot had straightened up, standing at attention like an evergreen army. Then, with perfect synchronization, they all exhaled. Thousands of pine needles released at once, creating a gentle green rainfall that sounded like nature's wind chimes.

The needles didn't fall randomly. They formed patterns on the snow: some spelled out "REST," while others created a perfect circle around Zoe's discarded lunch bag. A few particularly ambitious needles arranged themselves into what looked suspiciously like a "No WiFi" symbol.

"Did those trees just... stage an intervention?" The young couple stared as their potential Christmas trees nodded in unison.

Zoe's phone chose that moment to slip from her shoulder, landing in a soft pile of pine needles that had helpfully positioned themselves to catch it. When she picked it up, her color-coded schedule app had mysteriously closed, replaced by her phone's meditation app.

The Blue Spruce dropped one final needle, which landed squarely on her planner, covering up the words "midnight study session."

"Okay, okay!" Zoe laughed, holding up her hands in surrender. "I get the message!"

The trees rustled with satisfaction, and the lot filled with the scent of fresh pine—nature's version of a group hug.

"Umm," murmured Ryan, brushing needles out of his hair, "I don't think this was covered in our photosynthesis chapter."

The young couple ended up buying both trees ("When magical trees give you life advice, you listen"), and Zoe finally sat down to eat her long-forgotten lunch. The trees maintained a watchful presence, like a forest of evergreen guardians.

"You know," Ryan said, watching the needle shower, "my coach always says you can't sprint a marathon."

"Your coach sounds wise," Zoe's dad called out from where he was definitely not eavesdropping while pretending to organize wreaths. "Like trees!"

The Blue Spruce nodded emphatically, causing another minor pine needle avalanche.

That evening, as they were closing up, Zoe looked at her planner. Really looked at it. Between the highlighted deadlines and cramped notes, there wasn't any space for actual life to happen.

"Hey, Ryan?" she said suddenly. "Want to get hot chocolate? We can study for your test tomorrow, or... maybe just drink hot chocolate."

The trees practically danced with delight.

Over steaming cups topped with ridiculous amounts of whipped cream, Ryan admitted something. "I used to think I was just bad at chemistry. But maybe I just needed to learn it differently."

Zoe thought about her own rigid ideas of success, about how she'd been trying to grow as fast and straight as possible, never bending, never resting.

"Yeah," she said softly. "Maybe we all do."

The next week, Ryan got a B+ on his chemistry test—not perfect, but real progress. Zoe reworked her schedule to include actual breaks and renamed it "Flexible Growth Plan (With Optional Naps)." She even caught herself humming while working on college applications, no longer treating them like battles to be won.

And the trees? They kept teaching in their quiet way, dropping wisdom along with their needles. About how some days you grow, some days you rest, and some days you just sway in the wind and trust that you're exactly where you need to be.

✧

On Christmas Eve, as they sold their last tree (the Blue Spruce, to a family who swore it winked at them), Ryan helped close the lot.

"You know what's weird?" he said, sweeping pine needles into a pattern that looked suspiciously like a chemical formula. "I'm actually going to miss studying here."

"The trees will miss you too," Zoe smiled. "Even if they're terrible at spelling."

That night, Zoe added something new to her planner. Between AP Physics and debate team, she drew a little tree and wrote: "Remember to grow at your own pace."

Somewhere in the distance, a forest of Christmas trees whispered their approval.

And if anyone noticed that the Collin's Family Christmas Tree Lot became known for its mysteriously excellent study spots and surprisingly wise trees, well... that was just part of the Christmas magic.

After all, as Zoe's dad liked to say, "The best kind of growth happens when you're not checking its progress every five minutes."

Though he did admit that having trees that could teach chemistry was a pretty nice bonus.

CHAPTER 10
Reindeer Games at Rainbow Retirement

Ashley Parker stared at the craft instruction sheet like it was written in ancient Egyptian hieroglyphics. Which, honestly, might have been easier to understand than these supposedly "simple steps" for making paper reindeer decorations.

"Fold along the dotted... something," she muttered, turning the paper sideways. "Or maybe that says 'dated lime.' Why would a reindeer need a dated lime?"

The *Rainbow Retirement Home's* activity room sparkled with holiday cheer, though someone had gotten a bit overenthusiastic with the tinsel. Mr. Jenkins, a resident known for his creative decorating, had managed to turn himself into a human Christmas tree while attempting to hang garland.

"Need any help, dear?" Mrs. Wilson shuffled over, wearing a sweater that played "Jingle Bells" when you squeezed the reindeer nose. "Though I should warn you, my crafting skills peaked in 1962."

"I'm fine!" Ashley said quickly, hiding the instructions under a pile of red and green paper. "Just... adding creative flair to these reindeer."

Her "creative flair" currently looked like a paper deer having an existential crisis. Its head was where its tail should be, and its antlers resembled broken spaghetti more than anything found in nature.

That's when something odd happened. The tinsel on the wall behind her suddenly rearranged itself to spell out "FOLD RIGHT." When she blinked in surprise, it quickly transformed back into regular decorations, leaving her wondering if she'd imagined it.

"Oh my," said a familiar voice. "That reindeer looks exactly how I feel before my morning coffee."

Ashley turned to find Mrs. Henderson, her former third-grade teacher, now a Rainbow Retirement resident, wearing a Santa hat adorned with working fairy lights.

"Mrs. H? I didn't know you were here!" Ashley's existential crisis reindeer crumpled slightly in her hands.

"Retired last year," Mrs. Henderson winked. "Figured I'd join the cool kids. Besides, where else can you find impromptu Christmas carol karaoke at 3 AM?"

The fairy lights on her hat twinkled mysteriously, and Ashley could have sworn they blinked in a pattern that looked suspiciously like "LET'S HELP."

"You know what these reindeer games need?" Mrs. Henderson declared, adjusting her twinkling hat. "A story circle! Each craft tells a tale. No written instructions required."

The fairy lights danced excitedly, and somewhere in the room, a mechanical Santa started ho-ho-hoing in what sounded suspiciously like approval.

"But the volunteer coordinator said—" Ashley started.

"The volunteer coordinator also thinks fruit cake is a valid dessert option," Mrs. Henderson whispered. "Some rules are meant to be creatively reinterpreted."

Before Ashley could protest, Mrs. Henderson had gathered a group of residents, each armed with colorful paper and varying levels of crafting enthusiasm. Mr. Jenkins had finally untangled himself from the garland, though he'd kept a tinsel boa as a fashion statement.

"Once upon a time," Mrs. Henderson began, folding paper with dramatic flair, "there was a reindeer who couldn't fly in straight lines..."

The decorations around the room seemed to perk up and pay attention. Ornaments shifted to catch the light just right, creating helpful shadows that showed where to fold. The tinsel continued its helpful spelling, though it got a bit overexcited and briefly spelled "RUDOLPH RULES."

"This reindeer," Mrs. Henderson continued, winking at Ashley, "had her own way of seeing things. When other reindeer flew left, she went right. When they saw straight paths, she saw zigzags. But you know what?"

"She discovered breakdancing?" suggested Mr. Jenkins, whose reindeer now sported a tiny disco ball.

"She invented aerial ballet!" called out Mrs. Wilson, whose sweater had started playing "Jingle Bells" completely unprompted.

Ashley found herself relaxing as she followed the story rather than the written steps. Her hands seemed to know what to do when she wasn't stressing about reading the instructions. The fairy lights on Mrs. Henderson's hat created helpful patterns on her paper, and was it her imagination, or was the tinsel now doing interpretive dance?

"Actually," Mrs. Henderson smiled, "she became a master of finding new paths. And those zigzags? Turned out they were much better for avoiding air traffic."

By now, the activity room had transformed into a creative chaos of flying paper, laughing residents, and increasingly elaborate reindeer designs. Mr. Jenkins' disco reindeer had started a conga line across the bulletin board. Mrs. Wilson's creation was wearing a tiny replica of her musical sweater. And Ashley's reindeer... actually looked like a reindeer. A uniquely styled, slightly unconventional reindeer, but definitely recognizable.

"You always were good at finding creative solutions," Mrs. Henderson said softly to Ashley. "Remember in third grade? When you turned your book report into a puppet show?"

Ashley remembered. It was the first time she'd felt proud of a school project, instead of anxious about the reading parts.

The Christmas decorations were now fully invested in the activity. The tinsel had organized itself into clear, picture-based instructions. Ornaments rolled themselves into position to demonstrate folding techniques. Even the mechanical Santa had stopped ho-ho-hoing and was holding up surprisingly helpful gesture-based directions.

"Mrs. H?" Ashley said hesitantly. "How did you know? About... about the reading thing?"

"Teachers know lots of things," Mrs. Henderson's hat twinkled knowingly. "We also know that different isn't wrong. It's just... different. Like a reindeer who flies in zigzags."

Suddenly inspired, Ashley grabbed fresh paper. "What if we make the reindeer games actually games? Like, instruction-free crafts where everyone can tell their own story?"

The decorations practically vibrated with excitement. The tinsel spelled out "BRILLIANT" before catching itself and trying to look casual.

And so "Reindeer Games" became "Reindeer Tales and Trails"—an afternoon of storytelling, crafting, and what Mr. Jenkins insisted on calling "interpretive reindeer dance theater." Every creation was unique, every story valid, and nobody needed written instructions to participate.

Mrs. Wilson's sweater played "Jingle Bells" in triumph, Mr. Jenkins' disco reindeer led increasingly elaborate dance numbers, and the mechanical Santa finally gave up all pretense and joined the tinsel in spelling out encouraging messages.

Later, as they pinned their creations on the wall—creating what looked like either a reindeer modern art exhibition or a very festive fever dream—Mrs. Henderson pulled Ashley aside.

"You know what would make these games even better next week? If you helped design them. For all kinds of learners."

Ashley looked at her unconventional reindeer, then at the room full of happy residents and their wonderfully weird creations. "I'd like that. Maybe... maybe I could share some of my own tricks? For making things easier to understand?"

The fairy lights performed what could only be described as a celebratory dance. The tinsel spelled out "YES!" before quickly pretending to be normal decorations again. And somewhere in the back, Mr. Jenkins' disco reindeer started a conga line that would probably continue well into the night.

After all, as Mrs. Henderson's hat twinkled wisely, the best Christmas magic isn't about doing things the "right" way—it's about finding your own way to make the season bright.

Even if that way involves disco reindeer and sentient tinsel.

Especially if it involves disco reindeer and sentient tinsel.

By New Year's, *Rainbow Retirement Home* had gained a reputation for having the most unique holiday activities in town. Ashley's "Choose Your Own Adventure" craft sessions became so popular that they had to add extra chairs—and Mr. Jenkins insisted on adding a small disco ball "for ambiance."

The weekly Reindeer Tales and Trails evolved into different themes: "Snowman Storytelling" (where Mrs. Wilson's creation somehow ended up wearing a tiny musical sweater just like hers), "Elf Engineering" (Mr. Jenkins turned this into a dance party, naturally), and "Santa's Workshop Without Words" (where the decorations only occasionally had to restrain themselves from being too obviously helpful).

Ashley started bringing her school projects to Mrs. Henderson, who always seemed to have a creative way to approach them. Sometimes the fairy lights on her hat would arrange themselves into study guides, and the tinsel developed a habit of spelling out encouraging messages when Ashley least expected it.

"You know what's funny?" Ashley told Mrs. Henderson one day, while helping to take down the Christmas decorations (which were being surprisingly cooperative about the whole thing). "I used to hate asking for help. Now I'm teaching other kids my tricks for making instructions easier."

"And how's that working out?" Mrs. Henderson asked, as her hat twinkled knowingly.

"Well, Jenny from my Math class stopped crying during word problems, and Tim actually volunteered to read in English yesterday—using different colored papers like we do here."

The mechanical Santa, who was supposed to be packed away but had somehow escaped his box, let out a celebratory "Ho ho ho!"

"Though I still can't explain why the disco reindeer are now a permanent part of the retirement home's decor," Ashley added.

"Some Christmas magic is meant to last," Mrs. Henderson winked, watching Mr. Jenkins teach a group of residents his famous 'Rudolf the Red-Nosed Disco King' dance routine. "Besides, who says reindeer can't breakdance all year round?"

The tinsel, in its final act before being packed away, spelled out one last message: "DIFFERENT IS BRILLIANT."

And if anyone noticed that *Rainbow Retirement Home's* decorations seemed to rearrange themselves helpfully throughout the year, well... that was just part of the magic of finding your own way to shine.

Even the volunteer coordinator had to admit—though she still defended fruit cake as a valid dessert choice—that sometimes the best solutions come from thinking differently.

Especially when those solutions involve disco-dancing reindeer and mysteriously helpful tinsel.

CHAPTER 11
The Elf Workshop Emergency

Rachel Gibson was pretty sure glitter wasn't supposed to move on its own. Yet there it was, a sparkly trail floating through the empty hospital storage room, leading away from where the donated toys had been stored just hours ago.

"Well, this is just perfect," she muttered, adjusting her volunteer elf hat, which insisted on sliding sideways no matter how many bobby pins she used. "First Christmas in a new town, and someone steals all the pediatric ward's presents. Mom's going to love this update during our next video call."

The glitter trail swirled impatiently, like it was saying "Hey! Less talking, more following!"

Rachel checked her phone: 127 missing toys, 36 hours until the hospital's Christmas Eve celebration, and exactly zero ideas how to fix this. Unless...

"Did one of you come to life?" she asked the remaining toys—a lone teddy bear with a slightly crooked bow tie. "Because I could really use a Christmas miracle right about now."

The bear didn't answer (which was probably for the best), but the glitter trail suddenly sparkled more intensely, leading toward the hospital's main entrance.

"Following mysterious glitter," Rachel sighed, straightening her elf hat again. "This is definitely not covered in the volunteer handbook."

Outside, the December air was crisp, and the town's holiday decorations twinkled cheerfully, clearly unaware of the toy-related crisis at hand. The glitter path split into multiple streams, each heading in different directions through the small downtown.

One stream led to "Max's Hobby Shop," where a sign proclaimed: "Annual Model Train Exhibition—Today Only!"

As Rachel approached the window, the glitter formed three words: "GO IN ALREADY!"

"Bossy glitter," she mumbled, but pushed open the door, setting off a chorus of jingle bells.

Inside, she found organized chaos. Dozens of elaborate model trains circled miniature Christmas villages while children pressed their faces against display cases. And there, behind the counter, was a boy about her age wearing a conductor's hat and the same overwhelmed expression she'd seen in her own mirror that morning.

"Welcome to the madhouse!" he called out. "I'm Max. Well, Max Junior. Actually Malcolm, but nobody calls me that except my mom when I accidentally set the train displays on fire. Which only happened once. This month."

The glitter, Rachel noticed, was doing a celebratory dance around his hat.

"I'm Rachel," she said, watching as the glitter settled into the shape of a tiny train. "And this might sound weird, but... would you happen to have any toy trains you'd be willing to donate? Like, a lot of them? By tomorrow?"

Max's eyes lit up. "The hospital toys got stolen, right? Dad and I were just talking about that—it's all over the town's Facebook group. Which, by the way, is usually just people arguing about whose Christmas lights are too bright, so this is actually exciting news. I mean, not exciting-exciting, more like concerning-exciting..."

The glitter formed an exclamation point, as if telling him to get to the point.

"Anyway," Max continued, adjusting his conductor's hat, "we were already planning to donate the display trains after the exhibition. They're all new—we just set them up for show. Would twenty trains help?"

Rachel's elf hat actually stayed straight for the first time all day. "That would be amazing! But are you sure?"

"'Tis the season and all that," Max grinned. "Besides, my dad always says a train set is just a story waiting to happen."

The glitter twirled excitedly, then shot out the door, creating a new trail. Through the window, Rachel could see it leading to "Mrs. Chen's Craft Corner."

"Want some help?" Max asked, already untying his apron. "Dad can handle the shop, and I'm pretty good at following sparkly trails. Which is a sentence I never thought I'd say."

At Mrs. Chen's, they found a winter wonderland of handmade stuffed animals. The glitter swirled around a display of pandas wearing holiday scarves.

"The hospital toys?" Mrs. Chen nodded before they could explain. "Take these—I was making them for the holiday market, but this is better. And take some craft kits too. Kids need something to do while they're healing."

The glitter trail led them all over town: to the bookstore, where Mr. Patterson donated his entire stock of holiday stories; to the sports shop, where Coach Kim gave them dozens of foam balls and games; to the diner, where Annie the waitress organized an impromptu bake sale to raise money for more toys.

At each stop, people didn't just donate—they joined the mission. Max's dad brought his truck to transport everything. Mrs. Chen called her knitting circle, and soon there were dozens of handmade blankets. Even Mr. Rodriguez, known for being the town grump, contributed his entire collection of remote-control cars "They're cluttering up my garage anyway," he grumbled, but he was definitely smiling.

The glitter kept leading them to more and more people, until Rachel's phone was buzzing with offers of help from all over town. Her elf hat had given up trying to stay straight and was now jauntily celebrating at a permanent angle.

"You know what's weird?" Max said as they sorted donations in the hospital storage room. "Some of this stuff is even better than what was stolen. Like these train sets—they're actually nicer than the original donations."

The glitter, which had been suspiciously quiet, formed a small halo.

"Almost like someone knew exactly where to lead us," Rachel smiled. "Though I'm still not sure about that bear…"

The teddy bear with the crooked bow tie, now surrounded by new toy friends, seemed to wink.

✧

By Christmas Eve, the pediatric ward had transformed into a wonderland. Every room had personalized gift bags, craft supplies, and enough activities to last well into the new year. The train sets became part of a permanent play area, complete with a miniature version of their town (with extra glitter, at Max's insistence).

Rachel's mom called during the celebration. "How's the new town treating you, sweetheart?"

Rachel looked around at her new friends: Max teaching kids how to build train tracks, Mrs. Chen leading a stuffed animal parade, Mr. Rodriguez pretending he wasn't getting emotional over thank-you cards from the children.

"It feels like home," she said. "A very glittery home."

The sparkly trails had faded, but they'd left something better: connections, friendships, and the kind of community spirit that made even hospital corridors feel magical.

Later, as they were cleaning up, Max nudged her. "Hey, want to help with the hobby shop's New Year's exhibition? Dad's letting me design a winter wonderland display, and I could use someone who's good at following mysterious glitter trails."

"Only if we can add a teddy bear conductor," Rachel grinned, straightening her elf hat one last time.

The remaining glitter formed a tiny thumbs-up before dissolving into the air, its work complete. Though sometimes, late at night, visitors to the pediatric ward swear they see sparkly trails leading children to exactly the toy they need.

And if the teddy bear with the crooked bow tie occasionally rearranges the train village when no one's looking, well... every town needs its own special kind of Christmas magic.

Even the town's Facebook group agreed—between debates about excessive holiday lighting, of course.

As for Rachel, she finally understood what her mom always said about military families: home isn't a place, it's where you find your people. Sometimes you just need a little glitter to light the way.

And maybe a crooked elf hat that never quite stays straight but points you in exactly the right direction anyway.

CHAPTER 12
Mistletoe Market Miracles

Jessica Powell's booth at the Winter Market was definitely invisible. Or at least, she desperately wished it was. Standing behind her handmade display of holiday crafts, she felt exposed—like a Christmas tree with all its needles fallen off.

"You've got this," she whispered to herself, adjusting her display of hand-knitted scarves for the fourteenth time. "The shelter needs the money. Just... talk to people. Easy. Super easy. Totally—"

Her pep talk was interrupted by a strange shimmer in the air around her booth. The fairy lights strung across her table began to twinkle in an unusual pattern, almost like they were winking at her.

That's when something odd happened.

Britney Sanders, aka the Queen Bee of Jefferson High, was walking directly toward the booth with her usual entourage. Jessica's heart started its familiar drum solo of panic—but then Britney walked right past, her eyes sliding over the booth as if it wasn't there.

"Did we just... disappear?" Jessica asked her merchandise.

The fairy lights blinked twice, which she chose to interpret as "yes."

A moment later, Mrs. Martinez from the library approached, wearing her famous Christmas cardigan that played "Deck the Halls" whenever she sneezed. She saw the booth just fine, admiring Jessica's crafts with genuine interest.

"These are lovely, dear! Perfect for our shelter residents."

The booth remained completely visible to her, the fairy lights now performing what looked suspiciously like a cheerful dance.

"Thank you," Jessica managed, her voice barely a whisper. But Mrs. Martinez heard her perfectly, as if the booth's mysterious magic was amplifying just the right sounds while muffling the anxiety-inducing ones.

"You know," Mrs. Martinez said, examining a blue scarf, "sometimes the kindest hearts need a little extra protection while they do their good work."

The fairy lights chimed in agreement, and Jessica could have sworn the mistletoe hanging above her booth nodded sagely.

Throughout the morning, Jessica noticed a pattern. Kind people could see her booth perfectly, while others—like Tommy Thompson, who once made fun of her stutter during class presentations—walked past as if the entire display was cloaked in Christmas magic.

The fairy lights seemed to have developed personalities of their own. The blue ones twinkled encouragingly whenever Jessica managed to speak above a whisper. The red ones flashed warning signals when overwhelming crowds approached, giving her time to take deep breaths. And the white ones... well, they appeared to be running some sort of communication network with the mistletoe.

"Your booth feels so cozy!" said Emma Chen, a quiet girl from Jessica's art class who had always been nice but whom Jessica had never found the courage to really talk to. "It's like a little safe haven in all this market chaos."

The fairy lights preened at the compliment.

"Thanks," Jessica said, and found her voice was steadier than usual. "Would you... would you like to see how I make the scarves?"

The next thing she knew, Emma was sitting beside her, learning to knit. The booth's magic seemed to create a bubble of calm around them, muffling the market's overwhelming noise to a pleasant hum.

"I've always wanted to learn," Emma admitted, slightly tangling her yarn. "But my anxiety makes it hard to join groups."

Jessica's needles paused mid-stitch. "You have anxiety too?"

The fairy lights dimmed sympathetically.

"Are you kidding? I'm practically a professional worrier," Emma laughed. "Yesterday I spent twenty minutes practicing how to say 'hello' before coming to the market."

"I rehearsed my sales pitch in front of my cat for two hours," Jessica confessed. "She fell asleep."

They both giggled, and Jessica realized it was the first time she'd laughed at the market all day. The mistletoe above them scattered a few celebratory berries.

As the day progressed, their little haven attracted more people—but only the right people. Sarah from the school newspaper, who always stood up to bullies. Mr. Chen, Emma's dad, who brought them hot chocolate and didn't mind when Jessica took a full minute to say thank you. Even shy Kevin from the school band found his way there, his trumpet case covered in Christmas stickers.

"It's like the booth knows," Emma whispered, watching another kind soul discover them while a group of gossiping mean girls walked obliviously past. "Like it's creating its own little community."

The fairy lights spelled out "EXACTLY" in morse code.

By afternoon, something remarkable had happened. Their booth had become a quiet gathering spot for what Emma dubbed *The Gentle Hearts Club*. People taught each other crafts, shared stories, and most importantly, felt safe being themselves.

Jessica's anxiety didn't magically disappear—but it felt manageable, like a winter chill softened by one of her hand-knitted scarves. Every small interaction built her confidence, protected by the booth's selective visibility.

"The shelter's going to love these," Mrs. Martinez said, returning with more hot chocolate and an impressive stack of purchased items. "And I love what else is happening here."

She gestured to their growing circle: Emma teaching Kevin to knit, Sarah interviewing a elderly gentleman about his memories of markets past, two middle school girls finding friendship over tangled yarn.

"We're thinking of making it a regular thing," Jessica found herself saying, surprising herself with the steadiness in her voice. "A craft circle for the shelter. For people who want to help but need a quieter way to do it."

The fairy lights erupted in a twinkling standing ovation.

Later, as they packed up (having sold every single item), Emma helped Jessica count the proceeds. "This is amazing! The shelter can get new beds with this!"

"And maybe some craft supplies?" Jessica suggested. "For our new circle?"

"Our gentle hearts craft circle," Emma nodded. "Where the magic of invisibility only works on Grinches."

The mistletoe dropped a perfect circle of berries around their cash box in approval.

As Jessica walked home that evening, she noticed something extraordinary. The market's Christmas magic had left a trace—a soft glimmer that followed her like stardust. It wasn't about hiding anymore; it was about finding where she belonged.

The next week, the Gentle Hearts Circle met in the library's craft room. The fairy lights (which had somehow found their way there) still twinkled protectively, but Jessica needed their help less and less. Turns out, being yourself is easier when you find your people.

And if some folks never seemed to notice their quiet corner of Christmas kindness, well... that was just the mistletoe market's magic knowing exactly who needed to find their way there.

After all, as Mrs. Martinez's cardigan played during a particularly powerful sneeze, some of the best holiday miracles are the ones that help gentle hearts shine their light—even if it takes a little magical invisibility to help them feel brave enough to glow.

During one of their craft circle meetings, Emma nudged Jessica gently. "Remember how we used to both eat lunch alone? You in the library, me in the art room?"

"Now we just eat lunch alone together," Jessica smiled, untangling a particularly stubborn ball of yarn. The fairy lights dimmed to create a cozy atmosphere, like they were sharing secrets at a sleepover.

"With bonus stress-knitting," Emma added, holding up what was supposed to be a mitten but looked more like a holiday-themed sock puppet. "Though I'm pretty sure my scarf is actually a trapezoid."

The lights twinkled in what could only be described as giggling.

Their circle had grown but remained gentle. Tuesday afternoons became known for quiet conversations, shared snacks, and the occasional burst of Christmas carols when someone felt brave enough to sing. They celebrated every small victory: Kevin playing his trumpet solo for their small group before the holiday concert, Sarah raising her hand in class for the first time, Jessica calling the shelter directly to coordinate donations.

One day, Jessica arrived to find Emma had brought her sketchbook. "I've never shown anyone these before," she said softly, sliding it across the table.

Inside were beautiful drawings of their market booth, capturing the magical moments Jessica thought only she had noticed: the way the fairy lights danced, the protective shimmer in the air, the mistletoe's knowing winks. But more importantly, Emma had drawn the people—all of them slightly nervous but smiling, finding their place in their little haven.

"You saw it too," Jessica whispered. "All of it."

"Of course I did," Emma replied. "Gentle hearts see gentle magic."

The fairy lights formed a heart shape above them, and someone's knitting needles clinked in applause.

That evening, they all stayed late, sharing hot chocolate and winter wishes. Mr. Chen brought his famous cookies, Mrs. Martinez's cardigan performed a full holiday concert (thanks to winter allergies), and Kevin's trumpet joined in for a surprisingly harmonious rendition of "Silent Night."

"You know what?" Jessica said, looking around at her new family of gentle souls. "I think the market magic knew exactly what it was doing."

"Creating a Christmas miracle disguised as a craft circle?" Emma suggested.

"No," Jessica smiled, reaching for another cookie. "Creating a craft circle disguised as a Christmas miracle."

The fairy lights sparkled in agreement, and somewhere in the library, a sprig of mistletoe bloomed out of season, marking their space as permanently magical.

And if their corner of the library became known as the place where quiet hearts could always find friendship, well... that was the best kind of holiday magic of all.

SECTION 4: CHRISTMAS WISHES & WINTER WONDERS: Where Everyday Magic Sparkles

Picture this: Snow falling softly outside your window. Fairy lights twinkling in the distance. That feeling when anything seems possible.

These four stories are for dreamers, doers, and anyone who's ever felt that special buzz in the air during December—you know, when ordinary moments suddenly feel like scenes from your favorite holiday movie. They're about girls who aren't afraid to make their own magic, even when life gets messy and complicated (because let's be real, it usually does).

Coming up are stories about girls who are basically you—dealing with super-fun questions like "What am I doing with my life?" while also trying to figure out why their golden retriever keeps eating the Christmas decorations. They're about finding your path (or paths, because who says you have to pick just one?), creating your own kind of magic, and discovering that sometimes the best memories happen when you're completely, utterly lost.

These aren't just stories—they're permission slips to dream bigger, laugh louder, and add your own sparkle to the world. Because sometimes the most magical things happen when you're just being yourself, trying to figure it all out, with maybe a few candy canes and fairy lights along the way.

Whether you're stressing about the future, trying to hold onto childhood magic while everyone expects you to "grow up," or just attempting to survive December without your dog eating another Santa

hat, these stories are here to remind you that:
a) You're not alone
b) It's okay to not have it all figured out
c) Sometimes the best paths are the ones you make up as you go
d) All of the above (spoiler: it's definitely d)

Welcome to Christmas Wishes & Winter Wonders, where magic is real, growing up is optional, and there's always room for one more dream. Even if it involves a golden retriever in a Santa beard.

So, grab your absolute coziest blanket, put on those fluffy socks, and dive into tales where winter wishes have a way of coming true in the most unexpected ways...

Welcome to your next favorite holiday adventure.

The magic is waiting... and it looks a lot like you.

CHAPTER 13
Snowbound at Santa's Workshop

Lucy Gray didn't mean to get locked in the mall's Santa's Workshop display. Really, she didn't. But when your parents work double shifts at the hospital and your only company is a half-decorated Christmas tree at home, even a fake North Pole starts to look inviting.

Besides, the display window was way cozier than the food court where she'd been doing her homework. And if she sat just right, behind the mechanical elf that occasionally malfunctioned into doing the macarena, no one could see her.

"At least you guys are consistent," she told the animated polar bears, settling into her hidden spot after the mall closed. "Same routine every day, unlike some people who keep missing family dinner night."

Lucy pulled out her phone, scrolling through old family photos while the display's twinkling lights cast soft shadows. There she was, age ten, posing with these same animated animals, wearing the hand-knitted sweater her grandmother had made before moving to Arizona for her health. Back then, Lucy had been the queen of color-coded sticky notes, tracking her parents' schedules so they could maintain their Tuesday game nights and weekend dim sum traditions.

"Remember when we used to name all of you?" she whispered to the mechanical animals. "Dad always gave you terrible puns. Sir Polar Bearington the Third. Elfis Presley." She glanced at the now-familiar elf. "Mom would pretend to be annoyed, but she kept a list of the names in her phone. She probably still has it, not that we've had time to visit together lately."

Three years ago, before her parents both took positions at the new hospital wing, things had been different. Lucy still had the photo album to prove it: Mom teaching her to make dumplings, Dad attempting (and hilariously failing) to untangle Christmas lights, all three of them ice skating at the mall's indoor rink.

"I get it, you know," she continued, her voice echoing slightly in the empty mall. "They're saving lives. Kids like me get to have their parents home for Christmas because my parents are working. It's important. It's just..." She hugged her knees to her chest. "Sometimes I miss the little things more than the big ones. Like how Dad would make up stories about this workshop being a secret superhero headquarters, or how Mom always hummed off-key carols while wrapping presents."

That's when the first strange thing happened. The polar bears stopped their eternal wave-and-smile sequence and turned to look directly at her.

"Oh no," Lucy whispered. "No, no, no. I've finally cracked from eating too many solo dinners."

The mechanical elf spun around, its perpetual smile shifting into a look of concern. The fake snow beneath Lucy's feet began to sparkle and swirl, forming words:

"Sometimes the loneliest people need to see they're not alone."

The display window's glass frosted over, but instead of blocking the view out, it became like a screen. On it, images started to appear: Mr. Rodriguez from the bookstore, eating lunch by himself. Sarah from her math class, sitting alone at the bus stop. The new security guard, sharing his dinner with a stray cat behind the mall.

"Are you showing me... everyone who's alone tonight?"

The mechanical elf nodded solemnly, temporarily abandoning its dance routine.

The polar bears shifted, making space for Lucy on their snowy platform as more images appeared on the frosted glass. Mrs. Kim from the alterations shop, humming carols to herself while working late. The elderly man who always sat in the mall's coffee shop, stirring his tea endlessly. Even her own parents, taking separate breaks at the hospital, each looking at family photos on their phones.

"We're all just... scattered," Lucy realized. The fake snow swirled in agreement.

The mechanical elf suddenly perked up, its internal gears whirring with enthusiasm. It pointed to the craft supplies stored in "Santa's Workshop"—glitter paper, ribbons, and enough art materials to decorate the North Pole twice over.

"What am I supposed to do with those? I can't exactly fix everyone's loneliness with glitter."

The snow spelled out: "Want to bet?"

That's when the second strange thing happened. The display's backdrop, usually a static painting of Santa's Workshop, began to change. It showed scenes of people coming together: community dinners, holiday gatherings, simple moments of connection.

"Are you suggesting..."

The elf did its macarena dance in what was clearly meant to be an encouraging manner.

Lucy reached for her phone, then hesitated. "But I'm just a kid. Who's going to listen to me?"

The polar bears exchanged a look that clearly said, "humans can be so dense sometimes." One of them nudged a piece of paper toward her. It was a flyer for the mall's community board, advertising free event space in the food court.

"A holiday gathering," Lucy said slowly, ideas beginning to form. "Not just for families... but for everyone who needs one."

The snow sparkled enthusiastically, forming little exclamation points.

Using the craft supplies, Lucy began creating invitations. The elf, apparently a closet artist, offered surprisingly helpful design suggestions when it wasn't randomly breaking into dance. The polar bears managed to point out spelling errors, which was impressive considering they didn't have opposable thumbs.

By midnight, she had a plan. The mechanical animals had helped her create dozens of invitations, each personalized for the lonely souls they'd observed. The snow had even contributed by forming perfect calligraphy (showing off, if you asked Lucy).

"But how do I get them to everyone? I can't exactly walk out of a locked display."

The elf's eternal smile turned mischievous. It pointed to the mall's old-fashioned mail chute, normally just a decoration. As Lucy watched, it began to glow with the same magic that animated her new friends.

One by one, she sent the invitations through the chute. The elf did a celebratory spin as each one disappeared in a puff of sparkly air, finding its way to the right recipient.

"You know," Lucy said, watching the last invitation vanish, "my parents' shifts end at different times. But they both pass through the mall on their way home..."

The snow swirled into a heart shape.

When the mall security guard found her the next morning (the elf had helpfully set off the display's lights to get his attention), Lucy had a perfectly reasonable explanation about falling asleep while studying. If he noticed the mechanical animals winking at him, he didn't mention it.

Three days later, the food court transformed into a winter wonderland. Lucy had expected maybe a handful of people to show up. Instead, she found a crowd of familiar faces, all holding sparkly invitations.

Mr. Rodriguez brought books for a story corner. Mrs. Kim taught everyone to make origami decorations. The security guard's cat made an appearance, wearing a tiny Santa hat. Sarah from math class turned out to be a brilliant cookie decorator. The coffee shop man knew all the best carol harmonies.

And her parents... they arrived together, having arranged to sync their breaks when they got their invitations. Her mom was carrying hot chocolate for everyone, her dad had somehow found time to make his famous snickerdoodles.

"Lucy," her mom said, hugging her tight, "this is beautiful. But how did you know everyone needed it?"

Lucy caught the mechanical elf doing a subtle thumbs-up through the display window. "Let's just say I had some magical help."

The gathering became a weekly tradition. Different people each time, but always the same warmth. The mall management, noting the success, officially designated the food court as a community space every Thursday evening.

They called it *Winter Warmth Wednesdays* (the elf had insisted on alliteration). Lucy's parents rearranged their schedules to never miss it. The security guard's cat became the unofficial mascot. Mr. Rodriguez started a book exchange. Mrs. Kim's origami decorations grew more elaborate each week.

And if anyone noticed that the Santa's Workshop display seemed to change its animation sequence to match the gathering's activities, well... that was just part of the holiday magic.

Lucy still visited her friends in the display, though now it was just during mall hours. The elf had permanently added the macarena to its routine, much to the polar bears' apparent embarrassment. The snow occasionally spelled out gentle reminders: "Connection creates magic" and "Lonely hearts find each other."

As for Lucy's family dinners? They weren't always perfect, not with hospital schedules. But now they had a community to fill the gaps, and somehow, that made the solo meals feel less lonely.

After all, as the mechanical elf liked to demonstrate through interpretive dance, sometimes the best Christmas wish isn't for what you've lost, but for the courage to create something new.

Even if it takes some macarena-dancing elves to show you the way.

CHAPTER 14
The Christmas Star Project

Nina Ward could do advanced calculus in her sleep, but right now she was more interested in calculating the exact angle needed to hide her sketchbook when her parents walked by. The margins of her physics notes had become an art gallery of light patterns and star designs, each one carefully concealed beneath equations and formulas.

"A proper future engineer focuses on structural integrity, not aesthetics," her mom always said, sliding Nina's art supplies further back on her desk while prominently displaying SAT prep books.

But tonight, Nina had something bigger than margins to work with. The community center's holiday light design contest was accepting submissions, and she had secretly signed up. The grand prize: illuminating the town square for Christmas.

She waited until her parents' bedroom light clicked off before pulling out her tablet and accessing the 3D modeling software she'd been teaching herself. That's when it happened—her screen glowed with an unusual iridescence, and tiny dots of light began floating off the display.

"I really need to sleep more," Nina muttered, rubbing her eyes. But the lights didn't disappear. Instead, they arranged themselves into a miniature constellation right above her desk.

A soft voice, somewhere between starlight and wind chimes, whispered: "Some equations can only be solved with stardust."

Nina reached out to touch one of the floating lights. It danced around her finger, leaving trails of mathematical formulas written in glowing script—but these weren't like her textbook equations. These were the mathematics of aurora borealis, the geometry of starlight, the physics of how light bends through crystal.

The universe, it seemed, had its own artistic flair.

"This is definitely not covered in AP Physics," Nina whispered as more lights drifted from her screen, each one carrying fragments of what looked like Leonardo da Vinci's notebooks—if da Vinci had been obsessed with Christmas lights and had access to holographic technology.

One particularly sassy light burst kept rearranging itself into stick figures doing jazz hands. Nina was pretty sure it was mocking her perfectly organized desk, where her parents had helpfully labeled everything with "Future MIT Student" stickers. Even her coffee mug read "Engineers Don't Need Sleep, They Need Solutions."

"You should see my bedroom," she told the dancing lights. "Mom turned it into a mini NASA command center. She even replaced my constellation poster with a periodic table."

The lights swirled indignantly, forming a perfect replica of Nina's old poster—the one she'd hand-painted in seventh grade, before her parents decided art was a "distraction from her potential."

Nina touched the glowing image, remembering. "That was the same year Dad caught me designing light shows instead of doing my geometry homework. He said, 'Sweetie, dreams don't pay tuition.'" She sighed. "As if I couldn't love both math and art."

The jazzy light burst performed what could only be described as an interpretive dance of protest, spelling out "Why Not Both?" in a sequence that somehow combined the Fibonacci sequence with disco moves.

"You sound like Grandma Rose," Nina laughed. "She's the one who taught me to paint. Used to say that every engineer should learn art, if only to make their bridges beautiful." Her smile faded. "Before she moved to Florida, she'd help me build these incredible light sculptures. We'd calculate angles and power usage but also talk about how light makes people feel."

The constellation above her desk shifted, forming a delicate bridge that was both mathematically perfect and undeniably artistic.

"Okay, okay, I get the point," Nina said, pulling up her contest designs. "But unless you magical light beings can explain to my parents how the golden ratio applies to Christmas decorations…"

The lights suddenly froze, then zipped into a new formation. They were showing her something—famous images throughout history. The Parthenon's proportions. Da Vinci's inventions. Modern spacecraft designs. But in each image, they highlighted something Nina had never noticed before: the perfect blend of mathematical precision and artistic vision.

"Hold up," Nina sat straighter, her engineer's brain kicking into gear. "Are you showing me that some of the greatest scientific achievements…"

The lights sparkled in what felt like approval.

"…were actually enhanced by artistic thinking?"

The jazzy light burst did a celebratory somersault.

Nina grabbed her sketchbook, no longer hiding it under her calculus text. She started drawing rapidly, but this time with a new approach. Each artistic decision was backed by mathematical precision; each technical choice was guided by aesthetic intuition.

The lights danced around her work, occasionally nudging her pencil to adjust an angle here, suggest a curve there. The sassy one kept adding tiny sparkles to everything, which Nina had to admit improved the overall effect.

"You know," she said, watching her design take shape, "Mom always says art isn't practical. But you're showing me the physics of beauty, aren't you? The mathematics of wonder?"

The lights rearranged themselves into a perfect Christmas star—one that followed every law of physics while still managing to look like pure magic.

As Nina worked through the night, the lights continued their lessons. They showed her how snowflakes form in patterns that are both mathematically precise and naturally artistic. How the northern lights dance according to electromagnetic principles while creating the world's most spectacular light show. How the very stars her parents wanted her to study scientifically had inspired artists for millennia.

The jazzy light, apparently a show-off, demonstrated how the perfect timing of holiday light sequences could be calculated using the same principles as orbital mechanics. It then added a tiny light-show dance break, just because it could.

"Thanks for the disco interlude," Nina grinned, "but I think I'm finally ready to show them."

She looked at her completed design: a Christmas light display that transformed the town square into an interactive constellation. Visitors would trigger different light sequences based on their movements, each pattern following precise mathematical formulas while creating pure artistic wonder. She'd included all the calculations, proving how each aesthetic choice actually improved the installation's efficiency.

The lights swirled proudly around their protégé.

"Think it'll work?" Nina asked, saving her final design.

The constellation above her desk reformed into a scene: her parents, slack-jawed with amazement, watching her design come to life. Then, because the jazzy light couldn't resist, it added a tiny light version of Nina taking a bow while wearing a crown made of calculator batteries.

"Show-off," Nina laughed, but she saved that image too.

The day of the contest presentation arrived with a twist Nina hadn't planned for: her parents showed up. They'd seen the event announcement in her browser history (apparently, future MIT students shouldn't have secrets from their parents).

"We're here to support your... scientific demonstration," her mom said carefully, eyeing the art supplies Nina had spread across her presentation table. Her dad was clutching a "Science Rules!" banner that clashed spectacularly with the festive decorations.

Nina felt her courage wavering until she noticed something familiar—tiny spots of light dancing in the corner of her vision. The jazzy one was doing what appeared to be a motivational chicken dance.

"Distinguished judges and community members," Nina began, her voice steadier than she felt. "Today I'm going to show you how the mathematics of starlight can transform our town square."

Her parents' forced smiles froze as she pulled up her designs. But before they could object, the presentation took an unexpected turn. The lights from her late-night study session had followed her, and they weren't about to let their student down.

As Nina explained her calculations, the lights subtly enhanced her digital mockups, bringing them to life in miniature above her display. When she discussed the golden ratio, they formed a perfect spiral of twinkling lights. During her explanation of wave physics, they demonstrated light interference patterns that had the physics teachers in the audience leaning forward in fascination.

"By applying the principles of orbital mechanics to the timing sequences," Nina continued, while her jazzy light friend added a tiny but mathematically perfect light-dance demonstration, "we can create displays that are both energy-efficient and aesthetically stunning."

Her father's grip on his banner loosened slightly.

"But the real magic," Nina said, taking a deep breath, "happens when we stop seeing art and science as opponents."

The lights around her surged into action, creating a small-scale version of her full design. The town square in miniature, where constellations told stories through mathematically choreographed light sequences. Each pattern demonstrated a scientific principle while creating something undeniably beautiful.

"Did you calculate all these trajectories yourself?" one judge asked, adjusting his glasses.

"Yes, using the same software NASA employs for plotting satellite paths," Nina answered. "But I also used color theory to enhance the emotional impact. After all," she glanced at her parents, "what good is reaching for the stars if we forget to appreciate their beauty?"

The jazzy light chose that moment to add a tiny fireworks display, which technically violated several laws of physics but definitely improved the presentation's dramatic impact.

Her mom was squinting at the calculations projected on the wall. "These energy consumption figures... they're better than current systems."

"Because I used art to solve an engineering problem," Nina explained. "By making the patterns more visually appealing, we actually reduced the number of lights needed. Beauty became efficiency."

Her dad had gone very quiet, staring at a familiar pattern in Nina's design. "That constellation," he said slowly. "It's the same one you painted on your bedroom ceiling when you were seven. The one we made you cover up."

"Grandma Rose helped me with that," Nina said softly. "She taught me that sometimes you need an artist's eye to see what the equations are trying to tell you."

The lights swirled gently, forming a bridge between Nina's technical diagrams and artistic renderings. A bridge that looked surprisingly like the one she and her grandmother used to draw together.

"I don't want to choose between art and science," Nina told her parents. "I want to use both to make something wonderful."

The judges were huddled together, but Nina barely noticed. She was watching her parents, who were looking at her presentation with new eyes. Her mom was tracing the mathematical formulas with one hand while gesturing at the artistic elements with the other, her engineering mind finally seeing how they worked together.

Her dad had put down his banner and picked up one of Nina's sketches, comparing it to the technical specifications. "It's like da Vinci," he said wonderingly. "Art making science better. Science making art possible."

The jazzy light did a subtle victory dance.

When the judges announced her as the winner, Nina wasn't sure what made her happier—the chance to illuminate the town square, or the sight of her parents tearing their "Future MIT Student" banner in half and replacing it with a new sign that read: "Future Artist-Engineer."

The lights celebrated by creating a miniature replica of Nina's future: a workshop where calculators and paintbrushes lived in perfect harmony, and every equation came with its own light show.

After all, as the jazzy light spelled out in its final dance number: "Some of the best Christmas magic happens when you let your heart calculate the angles."

And if the town square's holiday display that year seemed to feature mathematically impossible bursts of starlight, well... sometimes the best designs require a little help from some illuminated friends.

CHAPTER 15
The Santa Cup Chaos

Rachel Jenkins had three great talents: scoring goals, making split-second decisions, and getting herself into ridiculous situations. Unfortunately, only one of those talents was useful when she accidentally volunteered to organize the school's first-ever Christmas charity soccer tournament.

"I just meant I could maybe help," Rachel muttered, watching her golden retriever, Referee, prance around her bedroom with one of her practice jerseys. "Not single-handedly create the 'most magical holiday sports event in school history.'" She mimicked Principal Wong's enthusiastic announcement from that morning.

Referee wagged his tail, somehow managing to look both sympathetic and amused. He had been there when it happened, technically making him an accomplice. After all, he was the one who'd started it all by stealing the microphone during the assembly.

Earlier that day...

"And now, regarding our annual holiday charity drive—" Principal Wong had barely started when a golden blur shot across the stage, microphone cord wrapped around its wagging tail.

"Referee! Drop it!" Rachel had jumped up from her seat, face burning as her dog led the entire faculty on a merry chase through the auditorium. Somehow, the microphone was still working, broadcasting Christmas music from Referee's collar speaker—a gift from Rachel's tech-savvy little sister that was proving to be a terrible idea.

"Deck the halls with bows of holly!" blasted through the speakers as Referee weaved through the chairs, trailing tinsel he'd picked up somewhere.

Rachel had finally caught him near the stage. "I am so sorry! He loves Christmas music, and my sister gave him this speaker collar, and—"

"Actually," Principal Wong had said, straightening his tie while Christmas music continued to play from Referee's collar, "this gives me an idea. We've been looking for a way to make this year's charity drive more exciting."

That's when Rachel had made her fatal mistake. Still holding onto a tinsel-covered, music-playing dog, she'd said: "Well, we could combine sports with Christmas spirit. You know, make it fun..."

Principal Wong's eyes had lit up like a Christmas tree. "Perfect! Rachel Jenkins will organize our first-ever Christmas charity soccer tournament!"

The entire school had erupted in cheers before Rachel could explain that she'd meant it as a general suggestion, not a personal volunteer statement.

Now, looking at the chaos of paperwork spread across her bedroom floor, Rachel watched Referee demonstrating his new favorite hobby: balancing a Santa hat on his nose while attempting to dribble a soccer ball.

"You know this is your fault," she told him. "You and your musical collar shenanigans."

Referee responded by pressing his collar speaker, filling the room with "Jingle Bell Rock."

"That's not helping!" But Rachel was already laughing. She grabbed her planning notebook—covered in soccer ball stickers and now featuring paw print decorations courtesy of her furry friend.

"Okay, Ref, let's make this the most ridiculous tournament anyone's ever seen. If we're going to fail, we might as well fail spectacularly."

Referee barked in agreement, accidentally activating his collar again. As "All I Want for Christmas Is You" filled the room, Rachel started writing, unaware that her dog was sneakily adding tinsel to her soccer cleats.

The Santa Cup was about to begin, and chaos had already scored the first goal.

Rachel's list was already spiraling into holiday madness:

THINGS THAT COULD GO WRONG:
1. Everything
2. Literally everything
3. Referee might eat the referee's whistle again

"Focus," she told herself, while Referee attempted to wrap himself in Christmas lights he'd somehow excavated from her closet. The dog's collar helpfully started playing "Let It Snow" as he tangled himself further.

Her phone buzzed with team registration messages:
Team Name Submissions:
The Mistletoe Marathoners
Prancer's Power Forwards
The Gingerbread Goalkeepers
Elfish Eleven ("Get it? Like selfish but... elfish?"—Tommy from Math class)
The Candy Cane Kickers
Bob (Just Bob. From Bob.)

"At least we have six teams," Rachel sighed, watching Referee attempt to dribble a ball while still wrapped in lights. "Even if one of them is just... Bob."

Her dad poked his head into her room, took one look at the lights-covered dog, and grinned. "Need a referee for your tournament?"

"Dad, no—"

"Because I just ordered a Santa suit with stripes! Get it? Santa... referee... Santaree!"

Referee barked enthusiastically at the terrible pun, his collar switching to "Santa Claus Is Coming To Town."

"I'm doomed," Rachel groaned, falling back onto her bed. "Completely doomed."

Her phone buzzed again. The team captains wanted to know if they could:

Wear bells on their cleats

Use presents as goal posts

Replace corner flags with giant candy canes

Perform a choreographed dance number at halftime

Add points for "Christmas spirit"

Bring reindeer

"No actual reindeer!" Rachel texted back quickly, having horrible visions of Referee chasing Rudolph across the soccer field.

Speaking of Referee, he had managed to untangle himself from the lights only to appear moments later wearing... was that her old elf costume from third grade?

"How did you even find that?" Rachel demanded. The dog's only response was to press his collar, filling the room with "Santa's Coming For You" in what felt like a vaguely threatening manner.

Her dad reappeared, this time with her little sister Emma in tow. "I've been thinking about the whistle situation," he said. "What if instead of a regular whistle, it played carols?"

"And," Emma added, already pulling out her toolkit, "what if the scoreboard had dancing elves?"

"And," her mom called from downstairs, "what if the team benches were made of gingerbread?"

"That's structurally unsound!" Rachel shouted back.

"Not if you use the right frosting ratio!" came the reply.

Rachel looked at her planning notebook, then at her Christmas-light-covered, elf-costume-wearing dog, then at her dad who was now practicing his "Santa referee" ho-ho-hos, and finally at her sister who was definitely reprogramming something that should not be reprogrammed.

"Fine," she declared. "If we're doing this, we're doing it full chaos mode."

Referee barked in approval, his collar somehow managing to play "We Wish You a Merry Christmas" and "Eye of the Tiger" simultaneously.

The next day at school, Rachel posted the official tournament rules:

THE SANTA CUP RULES:
1. All teams must have a Christmas-themed name (except Bob, Bob can stay Bob)
2. Festive gear mandatory but must not cause actual injury
3. No real reindeer (looking at you, Jessica from Biology)
4. Points awarded for:
    - Goals scored
    - Christmas spirit
    - Not getting tangled in tinsel
    - Successfully avoiding Referee's attempt to steal your Santa hat
5. Candy cane corner flags are edible but please wait until after the game
6. The dancing Santa referee's decisions are final (even if he gets his beard stuck in the goal net)
7. Halftime dance party is mandatory
8. If anyone brings real reindeer, you're responsible for any dog-related chaos that follows

As she posted the rules, Referee trotted down the school hallway beside her, somehow already wearing a tiny referee shirt over his elf costume, jingling with every step.

"This is either going to be brilliant or a disaster," Rachel told him.

Referee's collar started playing "Both" by headphone-sharing between "All I Want For Christmas" and "We Are The Champions."

Rachel couldn't help but laugh. Maybe chaos was exactly what this tournament needed.

The first practice was exactly the kind of chaos Rachel should have expected. The field looked like a Christmas store had exploded, with tinsel outlining the penalty boxes and battery-operated lights wrapped around the goals.

"Um, Rachel?" called Tommy from the Elfish Eleven. "Our uniforms might be a small problem." His entire team was dressed as Christmas trees, complete with working lights and star headbands. "We keep getting tangled together."

Meanwhile, Bob's team (still just called Bob) had shown up in plain jerseys but with reindeer antlers that lit up and played "Rudolph the Red-Nosed Reindeer" whenever someone scored. The problem was, they played the song for ANY goal, even ones scored against them.

Referee, living up to his name and role as unofficial mascot, was attempting to officiate while carrying a candy cane nearly as big as himself. His collar speaker had been upgraded by Emma to play a whistle sound effect, but it kept glitching and playing "All I Want For Christmas Is You" instead of signaling fouls.

"Dad!" Rachel called out desperately. "Little help?"

Her father jogged onto the field in his promised Santa-referee costume, complete with striped candy cane whistle. "HO HO HO! That's a holly jolly foul!"

"That's not even a real thing!" Rachel protested, but she was drowned out by the sound of both teams breaking into spontaneous caroling.

The soccer balls weren't helping either. Someone (Rachel suspected Emma) had wrapped them in sparkly paper with bows on top. Every time a player kicked one, it shed glitter and ribbon across the field. Referee thought this was the best thing ever and kept collecting the bows in his candy cane.

"Okay, new rule!" Rachel announced. "No more glitter on the balls! I can see Brian leaving a sparkly trail as he runs!"

"But I like being fabulous!" Brian called back, his Christmas tree costume twinkling.

That's when the sprinklers unexpectedly came on, creating what Rachel could only describe as a winter wonderland slip-n-slide effect. Players went sliding across the field, trailing tinsel and ornaments, while Referee chased after them with his ever-growing collection of bows.

Her dad blew his candy cane whistle. "Time for the halftime show!"

"Dad, this is practice! We don't need—"

But it was too late. Someone had connected their phone to the field speakers, and suddenly "Jingle Bell Rock" was blasting across the soccer field. The Christmas tree team started a synchronized dance routine they'd apparently been practicing secretly, while Bob's team formed a reindeer conga line.

Referee, not to be outdone, pranced through the middle of it all, his collar somehow managing to play a remix of "Silent Night" and "We Will Rock You."

Rachel looked at her clipboard, then at the chaos on the field, and finally at her dad, who was teaching everyone the "Santa Slide."

"You know what?" she said to no one in particular, "Maybe this is exactly what a Christmas charity tournament should look like."

She joined the dance party just as Referee started teaching the Christmas trees a new trick—how to play soccer while doing the macarena.

By the end of practice, they had:
- Three broken candy canes
- Enough shed glitter to decorate a small palace
- One slightly damp Santa-referee
- Six teams who had forgotten they were supposed to be competing
- A dog wearing more bows than fur
- And somehow, impossibly, the beginnings of something magical

As everyone helped clean up (which mostly meant following Referee's glitter trail to collect scattered decorations), Tommy approached Rachel with his star headband slightly askew.

"You know," he said, "I thought you were crazy when you posted those rules. But this might be the most fun I've ever had at practice."

"Even with the sprinkler incident?"

"Especially with the sprinkler incident! Did you see Bob's team? Their antlers were like disco balls when they got wet!"

Rachel watched as her dad helped detangle two Christmas trees who'd gotten their lights crossed, while Referee proudly showed off his new bow collection to anyone who would look.

Her phone buzzed with a message from Principal Wong: "Just checking on tournament preparations. Everything under control?"

Rachel looked at the field again. Her dad was now teaching everyone a dance move called "The Gift Wrap." The Christmas trees had figured out how to use their lights to signal plays. Bob's team was harmonizing with their antlers. And Referee had somehow acquired a tiny Santa beard.

"Absolutely," she texted back. "It's going to be unforgettable."

That, at least, was definitely true.

Tournament day arrived with a light dusting of snow that made everything look magical—until Referee decided it was the perfect consistency for rolling in, turning himself into what looked like a living snowman with a Santa beard and referee shirt.

"Attention everyone!" Rachel called out, her voice barely carrying over the sound of twenty different Christmas songs playing at once. "Please remember: goals scored while caroling count double, but only if you stay in tune!"

The field had been transformed into what her dad called a *Winter Wonderland Sports Spectacular*. Candy cane goals, tinsel yard lines, and somehow—Rachel suspected Emma's involvement—holographic snowflakes that danced around the players as they ran.

"First match: The Mistletoe Marathoners versus... Bob!"

Bob's team had finally embraced the spirit, showing up with bells on their cleats that played different notes as they ran. Combined with their light-up antlers, they looked like a musical Christmas stampede.

The games that followed were less soccer matches and more holiday performances with occasional scoring:

The Gingerbread Goalkeepers formed a kick-line every time they made a save

Prancer's Power Forwards kept breaking into "All I Want for Christmas Is You" during corner kicks

The Elfish Eleven's Christmas tree costumes now had built-in fog machines

And Bob's team had choreographed their goal celebrations to sync with their musical cleats

Referee was everywhere at once—stealing Santa hats, distributing candy canes to the crowd, and occasionally joining the game with his own soccer ball (gift-wrapped, naturally). His collar speaker had given up on playing whistle sounds and now just played victory music for every goal, regardless of which team scored.

Rachel's dad, in his full Santa-referee glory, had to be rescued twice when his beard got caught in the goal net during particularly enthusiastic calls. "HO HO HO, THAT'S OFFSIDES!" he'd boom, untangling himself while Referee helpfully added more tinsel to his predicament.

The halftime show turned into an impromptu all-team performance where even the spectators joined in. Someone had taught Referee to spin in circles while his collar played "You Spin Me Right Round (Like a Christmas Tree, Baby)."

By the final match, no one could remember the score. The scoreboard, thanks to Emma's modifications, was just showing different holiday emoticons and occasionally spelling out "BE MERRY!"

Principal Wong, watching from the sidelines with a mug of hot chocolate, hadn't stopped smiling all day. The charity donation box was overflowing, and the local news had shown up to cover what they called "The Most Festive Soccer Tournament in History."

The final whistle blew—or rather, Referee's collar played a jazz version of "We Wish You a Merry Christmas"—and everyone gathered at midfield.

"And the winner is…" Rachel's dad began, checking his glitter-covered scorecard.

That's when Referee made his final play of the day. He grabbed the scorecard in his mouth, ran through a spray of holographic snow, and led everyone in an impromptu parade around the field, his collar somehow playing a mashup of every Christmas song ever written.

Principal Wong took the microphone. "I think it's clear who won today—the spirit of Christmas! And thanks to everyone's generosity, we've raised enough money to fund the children's hospital's recreation room for the entire year!"

The crowd erupted in cheers. Someone started a snowball fight. The Christmas trees turned on their fog machines for dramatic effect. Bob's team's antlers played a celebratory light show.

"Rachel," Principal Wong said, approaching her with a smile, "I think we've found our new holiday tradition. How would you feel about making *The Santa Cup* an annual event?"

Before she could answer, Referee bounded up, now wearing a tiny crown made of candy canes on top of his Santa beard, his referee shirt covered in signatures from all the players.

Rachel looked at her dad, still untangling tinsel from his beard, her sister showing off the dancing scoreboard to the news crew, and all the players exchanging decorated soccer balls as souvenirs.

"I think," she said, scratching Referee behind his candy-cane crown, "that sounds perfect. But next year, maybe we should get Referee his own whistle."

Her dog's collar responded by playing "Same Time Next Year" (feat. Jingle Bells).

And so *The Santa Cup* became a cherished tradition, where the spirit of Christmas met the beautiful game in a glorious display of chaos and joy. Nobody ever kept proper score again, the performances got more elaborate each year, and Referee remained the undisputed MVP (Most Valuable Pup) of holiday sports.

As for Rachel, she became known as the girl who proved that sometimes the best traditions start with a stolen microphone, a musical dog collar, and the courage to let Christmas chaos reign on the soccer field.

And Referee? Well, he kept his title as *Official School Mascot*, though he never did learn to use a proper whistle. But then again, why would he need to? His Christmas carol remixes were much more fun anyway.

To this day, if you visit the school soccer field during the holidays, you might find traces of glitter in the grass, hear the faint sound of musical cleats, or spot a certain golden retriever teaching new players the art of dribbling while wearing a Santa beard. Just don't forget to bring a candy cane—it's Referee's preferred payment for referee services.

CHAPTER 16
The Polar Express Promise

Taylor Flores stared at her college applications spread across her desk, each one a different flavor of future anxiety. Yale wanted to know her life's purpose (she could barely decide on breakfast). Stanford asked about her greatest achievement (did finally mastering a TikTok dance count?). And MIT... well, MIT probably wanted her to solve world peace while coding a robot that could make perfect toast.

"I miss when the hardest decision was whether to leave cookies or brownies for Santa," she muttered, clicking another rejection-worthy draft into her digital trash bin.

Her room was a perfect metaphor for her current state of mind: One half covered in college brochures, SAT prep books, and a whiteboard counting down application deadlines. The other half still displaying her childhood collection of snow globes and a worn copy of "The Polar Express" that she pretended she'd outgrown but secretly read every December.

"Mija," her mom called from downstairs, "another college letter came!"

Taylor groaned. "Just add it to the 'Future Stress' pile!"

But when she finally trudged downstairs, what sat on the kitchen counter wasn't a college letter at all. It was a single golden ticket, shimmering under the kitchen lights as if it was made from actual starlight.

"Where did this come from?" she asked, picking it up carefully.

Her mom looked confused. "What ticket, honey?"

Taylor blinked. The ticket felt warm in her hands, and somehow smelled like hot chocolate and pine needles. In elegant script it read:
ONE WAY TICKET
THE POLAR EXPRESS: FUTURE PATHFINDER EDITION
DEPARTURE: MIDNIGHT, DECEMBER 23RD
DESTINATION: WHEREVER YOU NEED TO GO
PS: YES, THIS IS REAL (AND YES, YOU CAN STILL WEAR PAJAMAS)

"Mom, you really don't see this?"

Her mother glanced at Taylor's empty hands. "Mija, maybe you need a break from all those applications. You're starting to imagine things."

But Taylor wasn't imagining the way the ticket warmed her palm, or how the letters seemed to twinkle like tiny Christmas lights. She definitely wasn't imagining the small post-script that had just appeared:

PPS: DON'T FORGET TO BRING YOUR SNOW GLOBE. YOU KNOW WHICH ONE.

Taylor's eyes darted to her bedroom, where her favorite snow globe sat on her shelf. It was from her tenth birthday—the last year she'd been absolutely, completely sure about everything. Inside, a tiny train circled an even tinier Christmas tree, and when you shook it, the snow seemed to dance in time with a melody only the globe knew.

"I'm either having a stress-induced breakdown," Taylor told her reflection that night, "or..." She couldn't quite finish the sentence. Speaking the alternative out loud felt too much like tempting fate—or maybe like admitting she still believed in a certain kind of magic.

The snow globe sat on her nightstand, occasionally catching the moonlight in ways that made the train inside seem to move on its own. Next to it, the golden ticket pulsed gently, like a star with its own heartbeat.

Taylor checked her phone: 11:58 PM.

"This is crazy," she whispered, but she was already pulling on her favorite starry pajamas—the ones with constellations that glowed in the dark. She grabbed the snow globe, tucked the ticket into her pocket, and...

CHOOOOOO!

The sound came from everywhere and nowhere, filling her room with steam that smelled like peppermint and possibilities. Through her window, impossibly, magnificently, a train gleamed in the middle of her suburban street.

It wasn't just any train. It was the train—golden and grand, with "POLAR EXPRESS: FUTURE PATHFINDER" written in scrolling letters along its side. Steam billowed from its stack in shapes that looked suspiciously like question marks.

And there, standing on her front lawn in a conductor's uniform that seemed woven from starlight, was...

"No way," Taylor breathed.

The conductor appeared as an elegant elderly man with silver hair woven with actual starlight and a conductor's uniform that seemed to be made from the Northern Lights.

"Taylor Flores," he smiled, consulting a pocket watch that showed not time, but what appeared to be every possible future simultaneously.

"Sixteen years old. Currently juggling five college applications, three existential crises, and one persistent case of what we call 'Growing-Up-Itis.'"

"I... um..." Taylor clutched her snow globe tighter. "Are you really...?"

"Morgan Freeman? No. Though I do get that a lot." He winked. "I'm the Conductor of Crossroads. Navigator of Next Steps. Guide to the Great What-Ifs. But most passengers just call me Al."

"Al?"

"Short for Algorithmic Life-path Illuminator. But that's a bit of a mouthful for name tags."

The train huffed impatiently, its steam now forming little exclamation points.

"Shall we?" Al gestured to the train. "Your future is running on a rather tight schedule."

Taylor glanced back at her house, where her college applications waited like a pile of unfinished expectations. "Will I... be back in time?"

"Time?" Al chuckled. "My dear, this is the Polar Express: Future Pathfinder Edition. We don't follow time—time follows us. Now, ticket please?"

The golden ticket practically jumped from Taylor's pocket into Al's hand. It sparkled even brighter now, the letters rearranging themselves to read:

PASSENGER: TAYLOR FLORES
CURRENT STATUS: THOROUGHLY CONFUSED
DESTINATION: CLARITY (WITH A SIDE OF COURAGE)
BONUS FEATURE: COMPLEMENTARY HOT CHOCOLATE

"All aboard!" Al called, though Taylor was the only passenger in sight. "Mind your step—the first one's always a bit metaphysical."

Taylor stepped onto the train and immediately understood what he meant. The interior seemed to shift and change, like a kaleidoscope of possibilities. One moment it looked like a cozy library, the next a high-tech laboratory, then an art studio, then...

"The hot chocolate car is this way," Al said, leading her through carriages that couldn't possibly fit inside the train she'd seen from outside. "Though I should warn you—it has a tendency to match its flavor to your potential futures."

"That sounds..."

"Terrifying? Enlightening? Like something a stressed-out sixteen-year-old probably shouldn't drink before bed?"

"All of the above?"

Al laughed, the sound like bells on Christmas morning. "Perfect answer. You're already getting better at embracing multiple possibilities."

They entered a car that looked like what would happen if a five-star restaurant had a baby with Santa's workshop. Tiny mechanical elves—wearing bow ties and safety goggles—were mixing hot chocolate in beakers and test tubes.

"Your snow globe, if you please?" Al held out his hand.

Taylor hesitated. The snow globe had been her constant companion through every major decision since she was ten. Inside, the tiny train still circled its tiny tree, but now the snow seemed to move with purpose, forming patterns she almost recognized.

"Trust the process," Al said gently. "Sometimes we need to shake things up to see clearly."

She handed him the globe. Al studied it with his twinkling eyes, then carefully placed it on a golden stand in the center of the car.

"Now then," he smiled, accepting two steaming mugs from a particularly enthusiastic elf, "shall we see what flavors your future holds?"

The first mug tasted like mint and mathematics, with a hint of stardust. As Taylor sipped, her snow globe whirled to life, the snow inside forming complex equations that danced around the tiny train.

"Ah," Al nodded, "The MIT path. Quite a prestigious flavor."

In the globe, Taylor watched a slightly older version of herself in a lab coat, surrounded by holograms and robots. Snow-Globe-Taylor looked... busy. Important. Slightly caffeine-addled.

"She's solving something big," Taylor observed.

"The unified theory of everything," Al confirmed. "Though she still can't figure out why her socks keep disappearing in the dryer. Some mysteries transcend even quantum physics."

The scene shifted as Taylor took another sip. This time the chocolate tasted like paint and possibilities, with subtle notes of creative chaos. The snow in the globe swirled into vibrant colors, showing her teaching art to eager students, her classroom walls covered in masterpieces.

"But this is completely different from the first future," Taylor said, watching Snow-Globe-Taylor splash paint with joyful abandon.

"Is it?" Al raised an eyebrow. "Both versions of you are exploring the universe—one through numbers, one through colors. Both are creating something new. Both are, if you'll pardon the pun, drawing their own conclusions."

The train lurched suddenly, and Taylor's next sip tasted like deadlines and determination, with an aftertaste of breaking news. The globe showed her running a digital media empire, tackling stories that changed the world.

"Three completely different paths," Taylor sighed. "How am I supposed to choose?"

"Who says you have to?" Al produced a fresh mug that tasted like... everything at once. Sweet and sharp, simple and complex, familiar and strange. "Life isn't a multiple-choice test, Taylor. Sometimes the best answer is 'All of the above.'"

The snow globe erupted in a kaleidoscope of possibilities: Taylor the Scientist collaborating with Taylor the Artist on a revolutionary visualization project. Taylor the Journalist covering the story. Each version of her building on the others, creating something entirely new.

"But colleges want us to have everything figured out," Taylor protested. "They want our whole lives planned by age sixteen!"

Al's laugh filled the car with warmth. "Oh, my dear. Do you know how many times the average person changes their mind? Their path? Their passion? Even Santa switched careers—he used to be a professional cookie taster."

"Really?"

"No, I made that up. But it got you to smile, didn't it?"

The train whistle blew a melody that sounded suspiciously like "Believe" as they pulled into a new car. This one was filled with what looked like lost dreams—forgotten toys, abandoned hobbies, dusty "what-ifs" floating like cosmic debris.

"Many people think growing up means leaving wonder behind," Al said softly, picking up a worn teddy bear that still somehow sparkled with possibility. "They pack away their snow globes and their somedays, thinking that's what maturity requires."

"Isn't it?" Taylor asked, watching a group of origami dreams flutter past. "We can't stay kids forever."

"No," Al agreed, "but we can choose what parts of childhood to carry forward. Wonder. Curiosity. The ability to see magic in ordinary moments. These aren't childish things, Taylor. They're the very tools that help us build extraordinary futures."

The train whistle sang one final note as they returned to the hot chocolate car. Taylor's snow globe had settled into a gentle swirl, the tiny train inside now trailing stardust instead of steam.

"Time to head home," the Conductor said, handing Taylor her globe. "Though I suspect 'home' might look a bit different now."

"Will I remember this?" Taylor asked, suddenly worried the magic would fade like a dream.

The Conductor's eyes sparkled. "Check your pocket."

Taylor reached in and found her golden ticket had transformed into something new. It was now a small card that read:

REMINDER:
LIFE IS NOT A SINGLE TRACK
ALL PATHS LEAD TO POSSIBILITY
PS: HOT CHOCOLATE HELPS WITH COLLEGE ESSAYS

"One last thing," the Conductor said, producing a tiny silver bell. "For when you need to remember tonight. It only rings for those who are brave enough to believe in both their dreams and themselves."

As Taylor stepped off the train, the night air sparkled with promise. She turned to thank the Conductor, but the train was already fading, leaving behind only a trail of stardust and the faint scent of peppermint possibilities.

Back in her room, Taylor found her college applications exactly where she'd left them. But now, instead of seeing a pile of pressure, she saw blank pages waiting for her story—all her stories.

She picked up her pen and began to write:

"Some people might say you need to choose just one path. But I've learned that the most interesting journeys happen when you're brave enough to explore them all..."

The snow globe on her desk twinkled, its tiny train still circling endlessly, leaving trails of stardust in its wake. Outside, real snow began to fall, and somewhere in the distance, a bell rang—soft and clear and full of promise.

Taylor smiled, knowing that growing up didn't mean growing away from magic—it meant learning to create your own. She reached for her hot chocolate (which somehow still tasted like possibilities) and continued writing.

After all, she had a lot of futures to explore.

And somewhere, on a train that exists between reality and dreams, a Conductor smiled and made a note in her celestial logbook:

PASSENGER: TAYLOR FLORES
STATUS: FINDING HER WAY(S)
DESTINATION: EVERYWHERE
NOTES: REMEMBER TO CHECK ON HER NEXT DECEMBER.
SOME JOURNEYS ARE BEST TAKEN MORE THAN ONCE.

Taylor got into several colleges, each acceptance letter mysteriously accompanied by a packet of hot chocolate that tasted like adventure. She kept the silver bell on her desk, and on quiet nights, if you listened carefully, you could hear it ring—a gentle reminder that some kinds of magic never really end.

They just grow up with us.

FINAL THOUGHTS: YOUR STORY CONTINUES...

Dear Magical Soul,

So here we are, at the end of our holiday journey together. Maybe you're reading this curled up in your favorite spot, maybe it's not even December anymore, but I hope you're feeling a little more sparkly than when you started.

Remember our girls?
- Lily, who found her courage on stage
- Sophie, who turned her stutter into strength
- Nina, who proved art and science could dance together
- And all the others who discovered their own kind of magic

Here's the thing about their stories—they're not really endings. Each one is more like a beginning, a first step, a moment of realizing that magic doesn't have to be perfect to be real.

And your story? It's still being written too.

Maybe you're dealing with:
- Family changes that feel huge
- Friend drama that seems endless
- Dreams that scare you a little
- Doubts that whisper "not enough"

But guess what? Those aren't your endings either.

They're your middle chapters, your plot twists, your character development moments. And just like our holiday heroines, you're figuring it out one page at a time.

Remember:
- You don't need to have it all figured out
- Your path doesn't have to look like anyone else's
- It's okay to be both brave and scared
- Your magic is uniquely yours

So take what you need from these stories: Lily's courage, Sophie's voice, Nina's vision and all the little moments of brave girls being themselves.

Carry them with you like secret treasures, little reminders that you're not alone on this journey.

And the next time you see Christmas lights twinkling or snow falling or stars shining, remember this: You're writing your own story of magic and courage, every single day. And it's already wonderful, because it's uniquely, perfectly, amazingly yours.

Keep shining, keep growing, keep believing.
Your next chapter is going to be amazing.
With endless holiday magic and absolute faith in you,
Your Fellow Dreamer

> P.S.—And hey, if you ever need a reminder of your own magic, these stories will be here waiting. Because sometimes the best kind of Christmas spirit is knowing you're braver than you think, stronger than you feel, and more magical than you could ever imagine.

✧·° Your adventure continues... ·° ✧

ALSO BY THE AUTHOR

Short Stories for Teen Girls: 15 Feel-Good Tales About Confidence & Self-Esteem
(Perfect Gift Book for Ages 12-16 Series)

Discover more stories of friendship, self-discovery, and everyday magic in this heartwarming collection. Join fifteen incredible teen girls as they navigate the ups and downs of finding their confidence, standing up for themselves, and learning that being perfectly imperfect is exactly right. From first-day-of-school jitters to friendship dramas, from finding your voice to learning to love yourself exactly as you are, these stories remind every girl that she's braver than she knows and more amazing than she imagines.

With 10-minute daily readings perfect for busy teens, this companion book continues the journey of self-discovery and girl power that you loved in the Christmas collection. Because every girl deserves to see herself as the hero of her own story—not just during the holidays, but all year round.

Available on Amazon.

Visit Sarah Bennett's authors page to learn more about both books in the Perfect Gift series.

ABOUT THE AUTHOR

Sarah Bennett is a former high school teacher turned writer who believes every girl deserves to see herself in the stories she reads. When not writing, she leads writing workshops for teens and speaks at schools about finding your voice and owning your power.

She lives with her rescue dog, Luna, and an ever-growing collection of journals.

Printed in Dunstable, United Kingdom